FURBALLS AND FATALITIES

A TALKING DOG COZY MYSTERY

HEYWOOD HOUNDS COZY MYSTERIES
BOOK THREE

CARLY WINTER

Edited by
DIVAS AT WORK EDITING
Cover By
COVEREDBYMELINDA.COM

WESTWARD PUBLISHING / CARLY FALL, LLC

ABOUT THE BOOK

Nailing a murderer is difficult... but so is dealing with a cranky talking dog.

When the owner of Hammer and Nail Hardware is found dead, Gina's most loyal customer, Erika, becomes the prime suspect.

Despite having every reason to kill Molly Burton, Erika vehemently denies involvement and pleads with Gina to help uncover the real murderer. With almost all evidence pointing to Erika, Gina and her talking dog, Daisy, along with Deputy Trevor Hutchinson, delve into the secrets concealed behind the aisles of the hardware store. However, the clues they unearth leave them with more questions than answers.

Adding to the chaos, Gina takes in a bonded pair of dogs who prefer solitude. Daisy is determined to break them up, despite Gina's pleas to let them be.

As danger escalates, can Gina and Daisy hammer out the details and expose the true murderer?

PREVIOUSLY IN THE
HEYWOOD HOUNDS
COZY MYSTERIES...

In Dog Treats and Death:

When Gina Dunner's brother, Vic, is accused of murdering his ex-girlfriend, Gina isn't surprised. Living the life of a womanizing ranch hand with questionable friends and a lifetime of bad choices had to catch up with him at some point.

After the Sheriff announces she has the right man, Vic vehemently denies the murder. When he begs Gina to help prove his innocence, she attempts to puts her doubts aside, despite him being the last one to see the woman alive. She and her rescue mutt, Daisy —a sweet, yet sassy, talking dog—start sniffing around into their own investigation.

CHAPTER 1

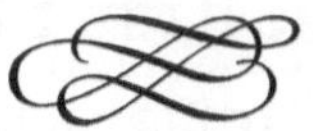

THE HOLIDAYS HAD PASSED, and I was sick and tired of being cold. As I turned up the heat in my nail salon, File It Away, I glanced out to see it was snowing yet again. Sure, Arizona had been in a drought, but enough was enough. At least I'd gotten to spend three weeks with my son, Jacob, who had come home from college. We'd watched all our favorite Christmas movies, had a big Christmas dinner with my father and brother, and Trevor also joined us. It had been a beautiful holiday season, but everyone was back to their normal schedules now.

Except my dog.

"Daisy, you're going to have to go outside

at some point," I said as she paced the length of the salon.

"I don't like my feet wet, and I don't like being cold," she muttered.

Considering she hadn't been out since the prior afternoon, I imagined her bladder was bursting at the seams. I worried about an infection. "Well, it's snowing again, so you better get out there sooner rather than later because the more snow there is, the wetter your feet are going to be and the colder you'll get."

She grumbled something while I pulled out my phone and glanced at my scheduling app. I swore when I realized my first appointment, Erika, was late. As one of my best customers, I could always count on her being on time. She worked as a checker at Hammer and Nail Hardware and absolutely loved to have her nails in top shape, mainly because she had a TikTok channel where she shared beauty secrets and makeup tutorials. According to Erika, one can't show someone how to apply eyeshadow with ugly, unkempt nails.

Twenty minutes passed, and so did my irritation. Worry took its place. It was highly unlike her to not show. Usually, if she was running even a few minutes late, she texted. I tapped my fingers against the counter while Daisy continued to pace.

I picked up my phone and sent her a quick text.

EVERYTHING OKAY? You're late for your nail appointment.

I STARED at the screen and waited for a reply. When there wasn't one, my concern only grew. It was even stranger for her not to answer my text. Erika was in her twenties and her phone was never more than a few inches away from her.

"Okay! Okay!" Daisy yelled, running for the door. "I can't hold it anymore!"

"Finally," I whispered.

After grabbing the leash and my coat, I left a note taped to the door and Daisy and I walked up Comfort Road a few blocks. I wasn't happy about being out in the cold, either, but I kept my thoughts to myself. Maybe I could teach her to use the toilet?

"There was a bunny here," Daisy said while sniffing the base of a tree.

"Do you need to go to the bathroom again?" I huffed, irritated with her exploration and worried Erika would show and I wouldn't be there.

"No. I'm done."

"Let's head back to the store."

When we arrived, Trevor was standing at the door dressed in his sheriff's parka, a baseball hat and gloves.

"Hey," I greeted him. "What are you doing here?"

"Trevor! Hi, Trevor!" Daisy exclaimed, her tail swishing.

The grimace never left his face, but it would have if he could actually hear my talking dog. She was excited to see him despite him ignoring her. "I need you to come with me," he demanded.

"What's going on?" I asked. After unlocking the door, we both stepped inside and I placed my phone on the counter then shucked my coat. "You seem like someone gave you decaffeinated coffee this morning."

A small smile turned his lips and he shook his head. "No, something far worse, although that would've been terrible. There's been a murder."

"Oh, no," I sighed while dread curled my stomach. "Who is it?"

"Molly Griffin."

"I don't know her," I said, furrowing my brow. Relief that I wasn't acquainted with the victim washed over me, followed quickly by guilt. I shouldn't be happy about the death, but instead, upset that someone had died.

"Well, Erika Roscoe does, and she's down at the station," Trevor growled.

"Erika?" I shrieked. "She's supposed to be here!"

"She's not going to be getting her nails done anytime soon," he replied. "She says you're the only one she'll talk to about her friend's death, so like I said, I need you to come with me."

Why in the world did Erika want to speak with me about a murder?

I rolled my eyes and shook my head. "Absolutely not. I've got a couple of appointments today. I don't see why Erika needs to talk to me."

"Gina"

"No, Trevor!" I yelled. "I'm not getting involved in any more murders! Erika can talk to *you*. You're the cop, not me. It's your dang job!"

He sighed, removed his hat, and ran a hand through his blond hair.

"You need a haircut," I said.

"I'm well aware," he muttered. "Look, you coming in and talking with Erika would help *me*, Gina. I've got a dead body at the hardware store and Erika isn't talking. Can you please just see what she has to say? As a personal favor to me?"

I stared at him a long moment while working my jaw. I was done with murderers, investigations, and all the stress that went along with these. A quiet life was what I wanted, free of all that nonsense.

"Please?" he begged. "It won't take much time."

With a curse, I turned and stomped over to the thermostat and lowered the heat, then grabbed my coat once again. "Daisy has to come with me," I grumbled. "And she's not waiting in the car. It's too cold."

"That's fine," Trevor replied.

"And I'm not talking to Sheriff Mallory," I spat. "Not one dang word, Trevor."

"She's on vacation," he said. "There's no chance you'll see her."

I nodded, my mood lifting a bit. Any day I didn't have to talk to Mallory was a good one. After grabbing my phone from the counter, I texted my two appointments. I notified them they'd have to come in an hour later, and I hoped the arrangement would work for them. Then I leashed Daisy. "Let's go."

"Thanks, Gina," Trevor said, placing his hand on my shoulder. "I really appreciate your help."

"Yay! We get to ride with Trevor!" Daisy shouted, her tail wagging a million miles per hour. "I love Trevor!"

Honestly, I hadn't heard Daisy meet one person that she didn't like. My dog was over-friendly, enthusiastic, and assumed everyone felt the same as her.

After locking up the store, I followed him to his truck. The snow was still falling and I cursed every beautiful flake while Trevor opened the door for me. Daisy jumped in and I followed. My teeth began to chatter as he hurried around to the driver's side. When he fired up the engine, the cool air blasting through the vents thankfully turned warm within seconds.

We drove to the sheriff's station in silence while I kept fuming because I'd agreed to talk to Erika. I had no idea who this Molly person was, but if she'd been found dead at Hammer and Nail Hardware, perhaps Erika had something to do with it since she was a checker there. I just wanted to remain blissfully unaware of the details, but it was too late now.

I was such a sucker.

Trevor pulled behind the Sheriff's Department, and I realized we were going in through the employee doors. Having never entered that way, my curiosity was piqued. I was going to see something new—the inner workings of the department. Even during my time as a resident when I'd been accused of killing my deadbeat ex-husband I hadn't been privy to this section.

Daisy and I followed Trevor inside through a locker room which held ten gray lockers, a couple of matching benches and a mirror. Once he opened the door leading into the main station, the odor of cleaning products and vomit greeted us along with the drab gray walls and floors. Placing my hand over my mouth, I'd forgotten just how depressing the station was. A splash of red or orange would really liven it up.

"Yuck," Daisy said. "What's that smell? It's burning my super sniffer!"

"Mine too," I muttered.

"What?" Trevor asked.

"Nothing. Why does it smell like barf in here?"

"A couple drunks were brought in last night," Trevor replied. "They had more than their fair share. It's been cleaned up, but sometimes the smell hangs around for a bit."

Maybe the sheriff's station didn't need to be livened up. It was probably best it wasn't since they were bringing in people already in different states of agitation.

He led us down the hallway and stopped at a room with a closed door, then turned to me. "She's in here. You can find out whatever she knows and then report back to me."

"Aren't you being a bit bossy?" Daisy asked. "Gina doesn't like being told what to do."

My dog wasn't wrong. I narrowed my gaze. "Maybe a "please" would be nice, deputy. Quit ordering me around. I don't work for you, and I'm only here because you asked quite nicely earlier."

"Sorry," he sighed, placing his hands on his hips. "Just stressed out about this. Please let me know what she says about her friend, okay?"

"Don't you have a camera or something in there?" I asked. "Record it, so I don't have to try to remember everything."

"Yeah, we'll record it, but sometimes the camera doesn't pick up all that's said."

I glanced down at Daisy, not sure what to do with her.

"I want to go in!" Daisy yelled. "I promise I'll be a good girl! Please don't leave me out here with the pukers!"

"Daisy's going in with me," I stated. Hopefully, I left him no choice. He stared at me a long moment. "Erika loves Daisy," I continued. "She'll bring her comfort and maybe if she's relaxed, she'll talk more."

Trevor hesitated for another moment, then nodded. "I'll see you in a bit."

As he hurried down the hallway, I opened the door. Erika sat at the gray table. Black mascara streaks lined her face. Her usually perfect black hair hung in oily, tangled strands around her shoulders. The gray walls and her black shirt paled her cheeks, making her look sickly. At least she wasn't cuffed.

"Daisy!" she yelled. I let go of the leash and Daisy ran over to her.

"Erika! Pet me, Erika!" Daisy demanded. The woman obliged.

With a long sigh, I slipped out of my coat, laid it over the back of the chair, and sat down across from her. I glanced up at the corner of the room and located the camera. Hopefully, the dang thing was working. Then, I waited while she whispered sweet nothings to Daisy. It had been smart to bring the canine in with me. Erika smiled and the stress seemed to seep out of her as her shoulder sagged. Dogs—the best therapists around.

Erika's black shirt quickly became coated with Daisy's white hair. How the dang dog wasn't bald, I had no idea.

"So, what happened with your friend, Molly?" I asked.

Her smile faded as she sat upright and turned toward me. Tears welled in her eyes and she shook her head as Daisy trotted back to my side of the table and lay down over my feet. I hoped no one had lost their stomach contents in this room, or I'd probably have to bathe her when I got home—a task both of us detested.

"Erika?" I said, my voice softer this time. "What happened with Molly?"

She swiped at her cheeks. "Well, first of all, she's not my friend, Gina. I hated her."

CHAPTER 2

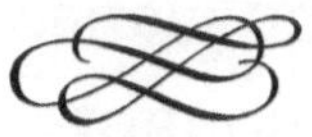

"CAN YOU TELL ME ABOUT HER?" I asked, now confused. Trevor had referred to Molly as Erika's friend, but it seemed that wasn't the case... according to Erika.

"Molly was Lewis' wife," she sniffed. "He owns the hardware store. They bought it a few years ago. Remember?"

I was in and out of the building multiple times a week. Being a single mom, I'd become quite proficient in household repairs throughout the years. Besides that, the hardware store had some really cute dog toys. I never paid much attention to who the owner was, though.

"Okay, so Molly wasn't your friend, but

the owner's wife. I'm still not sure why you're sitting in an interrogation room at the sheriff's department and you won't talk to Deputy Hutchison."

Erika sighed and glanced up at the ceiling as if to gather her thoughts, then met my gaze. "Okay, here's the deal. I got hired right after Lewis bought the store. I didn't even know he was married, Gina. That woman never stepped foot into the place until a few months ago."

I shrugged, still confused. "And?"

"She came in and started going through everything," Erika continued. "The books, the employee files, inventory... everything. It was like she was suddenly in charge and she had plans to make big changes."

"Well, she owns the store, so I guess I can understand that," I said.

"But she was never there beforehand," Erika insisted. "I didn't even know the woman existed!"

"Maybe Lewis asked her to come in and help him out," I said, shrugging, still unsure of why Erika wouldn't talk to Trevor. "Or maybe, she finally had time to work in the business instead of raising kids or something like that."

Erika shook her head as she stared at her nails. I'd painted them bright red with green and white rhinestones for Christmas. Two were chipped and her real nail beds showed at the cuticles. "No, this was something different. I can't explain it, but it was like a takeover."

"What did Lewis say about it all?" I asked.

"They fought a lot," Erika replied. "One time I heard him tell her to get out of his hair, but she said she had every right to be there and to see where the business was financially."

"She was correct," I said.

"I suppose you're right, but then she wanted to start making cuts. Inventory was falling low because she didn't want to order. She also... she fired me, Gina." Tears fell down her cheeks again.

"Why?"

"She said it was because of my TikTok channel."

I furrowed my brow and crossed my arms over my chest. "Explain this to me like I'm five, Erika. Why in the world would she care about your TikTok channel?"

Erika sighed and angrily swiped at her cheeks again. "Because I used to make videos in the store after-hours, and she said her store wasn't my playground to make and upload stupid stuff."

Pursing my lips, I hope I hid my smile. "What type of videos were you making?"

"Well, as you know, I produce makeup videos, but then I decided that girls my age who live alone need to know how to do basic repairs. So, I started showing them how to do things, like what equipment to use to unclog a sink, or how to fix a leaky faucet. We weren't shown how to do these things when we were growing up, so a lot of people get out on their own and don't even know how to change a lightbulb."

Rolling my eyes, I said, "You've got to be kidding me."

"No, I'm not, Gina. I actually made a video about changing lightbulbs because someone left a comment on my garage disposal repair series that they didn't know how to do it and were too embarrassed to admit it!"

I almost laughed, but then realized that such a channel would've been helpful when I was trying to figure out home repairs while raising my son. Money had been so tight, I only hired people when absolutely necessary. My brother and father helped out quite a bit and taught me a lot, but I'd hated relying on them and always attempted to repair things first before calling them in.

Erika's channel was actually doing a service.

"Okay," I sighed. "So, why did she fire you for the videos? Were you making them without permission?"

She shook her head. "Lewis had given me permission to do them as long as I mentioned the store once or twice during the video. He looked at them as free advertising."

But with TikTok being a worldwide platform, I wasn't sure how "free advertising" would play out for some little hardware store deep in the Arizona mountains. Maybe they had an online presence I wasn't aware of? But why would anyone order something from a hardware store across the country, or the world, when every community I'd ever seen had one?

"Did you mention to Molly that Lewis had given you permission?" I asked.

"Yes, I did. She said that it was all stupid and she wasn't having any of it in *her* store."

"She didn't give you the option of stopping the filming? She just automatically fired you?"

Erika pursed her lips and nodded. I was beginning to dislike Molly, even though I felt horrible she'd been murdered. Was firing Erika for making videos even legal, especially since Lewis had given her the go-ahead?

I'd thought coming in here would help Trevor solve the case, but I only found myself confused and now I worried about Erika. The poor girl was out of a job and the whole reason seemed sketchy to me.

"When were you let go?" I asked.

"Yesterday, just before closing."

"Did anything significant happen before then?"

"I heard Lewis and Molly fighting, and I

heard them shouting about lowering the number of employees."

"But they didn't say who, right?"

Erika shook her head. "Not that I heard, but it was obvious they were going to fire someone."

"Did you feel the store was overstaffed?"

"No, it's not," she replied. "I've had ten hours of overtime just this week. If anything, Lewis should've hired another checker."

I stared at her for a long moment. Erika was usually so put together with every hair in place, her makeup done with care and perfection, but sitting across from me, she looked like a trainwreck. Especially her eyebrows. I always knew she drew them on, but they'd somehow become smudged and crawled halfway up her forehead. She seemed terribly distraught. "Walk me through yesterday afternoon," I said.

"Well, I guess it was around two or three when they were fighting about the number of employees," she replied. "We were closing at six, so I just tried to mind my own business and do my job. At about five-thirty, Molly said she wanted to speak to me in the back office, and I knew I was the one to go."

"Where was Lewis?" I asked.

"He saw her lead me into the office and he shook his head, then turned away."

"So, it sounded like he didn't want you fired."

"That's the impression I got."

"Okay, you had your talk with Molly, and did you leave then?"

"I did. I was so upset I could barely see straight."

"Where did you go?"

"I went home, but then I went back to the store later, hoping to talk to Lewis. I mean, he's been my boss for all these years, so I was thinking I could have him talk Molly out of firing me."

"And was he there?"

She shook her head. "Lewis wasn't, but Molly was."

"What happened?" I asked.

"Well, as I was walking to the back office, I thought I heard her voice and a man's, which I assumed to be Lewis, and I was hopeful that maybe I could convince them not to fire me. I bumped into a display of car fresheners and knocked it over, so I quickly cleaned it up then headed back. But when I got to the office, it was only Molly."

"There wasn't anyone else there?" I asked.

"No, not that I saw at that moment."

"And did you talk to Molly?"

"I begged her not to fire me," Erika said, her voice cracking. "I told her I would quit doing the videos and I pointed out my till was always perfect and I helped with inventory without even being asked."

"She didn't budge, did she?"

Erika shook her head. "No. She said I should've been fired a long time ago."

Daisy laid her head on my lap and said, "Gina, I want to leave now. This place is depressing."

I thoroughly agreed, so I reached down and slowly stroked her soft head but kept my attention on Erika. "What happened then?"

A long stretch of silence filled the gloomy room, and I held my breath, wondering if Erika was going to confess to the killing.

"I got really mad," she whispered. "And I said a bunch of stuff I shouldn't have."

"Like what?"

"That Molly was an ugly, hateful cow."

With a snort, I slapped my hand over my mouth. And I thought I had a problem keeping my thoughts to myself! After a moment, I said, "Way to keep it professional."

"I know, Gina. I know. I said some other things as well... and then I left."

"Did you happen to say something about killing Molly?"

"I may have wished her dead, or something to that effect."

Muttering a curse, I glanced up at the camera. Things weren't looking good for Erika.

"But here's the weird thing, Gina," she continued. "When I was leaving, I swear I saw a man standing in the shadows at the end of the hall."

I narrowed my gaze. "Why do you think he was standing in the shadows? Do you think it was Lewis?"

"Who knows?" She sighed. "Maybe he didn't want to face me and was leaving the dirty work to Molly."

As I continued to stroke Daisy's head, I

became more intrigued. "Are you sure you saw someone there?"

"I'm like fifty percent sure," she replied. "But I was so mad, maybe I was just seeing things."

"Where did you go after your altercation with Molly?"

"I went home."

Dang it. I'd hoped she'd been at the coffee shop or bar for the night.

"Why did you want me to come here?" I asked. "Why won't you talk to Trevor?"

She leaned her elbows on the table, her gaze pleading. "I'm scared they're going to think I did it, Gina. I was fired that day, and I went back to the store. I have a motive."

I studied the scared woman in front of me. Yes, she did have motive to kill Molly, but it was a weak one. "Did you volunteer to come here today?" I asked.

"No. A deputy showed up at my house and dragged me here."

"Trevor did that to you?"

She shook her head. "Another guy."

"And why do they suspect you?" I asked.

"Because one of the other employees

heard me call Molly a cow a few days ago when she was yelling at me about something and he told the police about it. So, they brought me in for questioning."

"You and Molly had words before last night?"

"Yes."

With a long sigh, I rubbed my temples with my forefingers, trying to ward off the headache forming there. "You probably could've been gone long ago if you'd just talked to Trevor."

"I know what Mallory is like," Erika shot back. "I've watched her try to put a lot of people in jail who didn't belong there, including you, Gina."

"But she's out of town," I replied. "You don't have to deal with her."

Her eyes widened in surprise. "I didn't know that."

With a nod, I stood. "Let me talk to Trevor, okay?"

"I feel so stupid," she whispered.

"It's okay. I know from experience being in this building is scary, and when you have a moron in charge, it's every bit more frightening." I placed my hand over hers. "It's going to be okay, Erika."

After grabbing Daisy's leash, I left the room. Trevor waited for me in the hall.

"Did you get what you needed?" I asked. "I hope that camera was on."

"I did. Thanks. Do you want a cup of coffee before I take you back?"

"Sure." I hitched my thumb over my shoulder as we walked down the hall. "Cut her loose, Trevor. She's done nothing."

"That's what it sounds like." He led me into the small break room, poured a cup of coffee and handed it to me. "Fresh off the press."

We sat down at the small table and I sipped the horrid brew. I'd always heard cop coffee was awful, but this was even worse than my brother's. "How did Molly die?"

"She was beaten over the head with a hammer," Trevor said. "A pink one, to be exact."

"I didn't know they made pink hammers."

"Me neither, but Hammer and Nail have

pink, yellow and green, so they're really stepping up their game."

"Trevor, phone call line two," sounded from the speaker system overhead.

"I'll be right back," he grumbled.

While I waited, I pulled out my phone and opened TikTok.

"Gina," Daisy whined. "I want to go."

"I do too, but we're going to have to wait a minute."

I scrolled down and did a quick search, finding Erika's account.

The first video was of her lying under a sink with a wrench. "You want to make sure the water is off before you start any repairs under the sink," she said. Glancing over at the camera, she smiled and continued, "I mean, you don't want to ruin a perfectly good makeup job with water shooting in your face, right?"

With a smirk, I continued my scrolling through her channel. My chest turned icy cold as the next one started. Erika held a pink hammer in one hand and a nail in the other. "So, when you nail something into a wall, you want to hit the head of the nail firmly, while avoiding your fingertips. You don't want to ruin your pretty nails." She turned to a piece of wood hanging from the wall, placed the nail, and gently tapped at first. "You want to barely hit it at first so it has a chance to get lodged in there." I jumped when she then slammed it. "Once it's set, just think of someone who did you wrong and pretend you're hitting them on the head."

CHAPTER 3

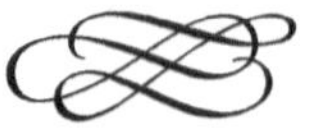

WITH A CURSE, I dropped my phone on the table and placed my head in my hands. What the heck had I just watched? Was it a huge coincidence that Erika had made a video just two weeks ago using a pink hammer and mentioning that one should bang a nail as if they were hitting someone who'd done them wrong, and now the person who fired her was dead... killed with a pink hammer?

And should I tell Trevor about it? I had to assume he'd see it eventually.

"Gina? Can we go back to the nail salon yet?" Daisy asked. "I can tell you're upset, and I don't like it. Let's leave and your mood will get better!"

If only it were that easy.

"In a bit," I said. "We have to wait for Trevor."

"But why?" she asked. "We can just leave and walk back. You have two legs and I have four. Last time I checked all of them were working right."

She had a point. It wasn't like I was being detained, but that weather sure made me feel like I was trapped. "Even if it's snowing and cold?"

"Yes. Even then. I don't like it here."

I picked up my phone to check the time. I still had a while before my next nail appointment, so I decided to wait a few more minutes to see if I could hitch a ride back with Trevor and dive deeper into Erika's TikTok channel.

The first video shown to me had been made yesterday.

"I've been fired," Erika said, her tears flowing freely. "I'm so upset because I don't think I deserved it. One of the owners said she didn't want me making these videos any longer... these videos that help *you*." She shook her head and looked away from the camera for a second, then back again and tossed the black curtain of hair over her shoulder. "Should I fight it? I need my job, but I'm so angry right now. Let me know what you think."

I glanced through some of the comments, and the consensus was that she should try to get her job back. Was that when she returned to the store? It had been posted seventeen hours ago, so the timing was tricky. I didn't have the exact hour she'd confronted Molly after the store closed.

In a couple of other videos, she showcased different tools in the store and explained what they were used for. Further back on the timeline, I ran into her makeup tutorials. For a second, I thought I had somehow stumbled onto someone else's channel, but then I realized Erika looked very, very different without makeup. I barely recognized her. "That's some witchcraft right there," I muttered, thoroughly impressed. I was lucky if I got my mascara on without stabbing myself in the eye.

I scrolled back to the more recent videos and clicked on one featuring Erika with a man standing behind her. She smiled and glanced over her shoulder at him. "Everyone, this is Nick. Isn't he cute?"

He laughed and nuzzled his cheek against hers. Sparkling brown eyes indicated he was pretty happy with Erika, as did his huge grin. She ran her fingers through the mop of his brown hair. "I think I'll keep him," she said. The video ended with them kissing.

I studied a few more of the two lovebirds, finding it strange as I always did when people lived out their lives online for the whole world to see. I'd watched couples fight and threaten each other with a divorce over Facebook, and don't get me started on the oversharing I'd seen on Twitter.

Another thumbnail showed Erika in tears, so I played the video.

"I don't know about Nick," she said. "Is he in love with me and overprotective, or is he overbearing?" She shook her head, then dove into a story about how he'd come to see her at work and found her talking with another man. It turned out they both knew the same person who had moved to Texas, so they were excited to exchange stories and update each other on what that person was now doing.

"Nick got so mad," she sniffed. "He told me I shouldn't spend so much time talking to other men, that I'm *his*. I don't know if that's love... or something else."

"That's a controlling jerk and you need to run," I muttered, searching for other videos of the two, or her being upset.

I found another of her, but this time she was angry. "I swear, I don't know what to do with Nick," she seethed. "Last night we were out to dinner and some guy tripped and bumped into me. Nick lost it and tried to fight him. Thankfully, he calmed down. He said that he'd always take steps to right the person who had done me wrong. Is that weird?"

"Jeez, Erika," I said into the empty room. "Are you really this dumb, or am I just that old that I can spot a bad apple from a mile away?"

The breakroom door opened and I glanced over my shoulder to find Trevor walking in. "Sorry about that," he grumbled.

"No worries."

He sat down and gestured to my coffee cup. "You didn't like it?"

"Not really." I shrugged and decided to show him Erika's videos. "I figured you'd find these sooner or later."

I pressed play and turned my screen toward him. His eyes widened when she slammed the pink hammer against the nail. "Well, that's interesting."

"Agreed, but not as interesting as this." I played the two videos of Erika complaining about Nick.

Once finished, Trevor let out a slow whistle and sat back in his chair. "Do you think she went home upset, headed back to the store to try to win her job back and then when she didn't, she told Nick about it?"

"And he lost his marbles and went and killed Molly," I finished for him. "I think it's definitely something that needs to be looked into. As far as I can tell from these little snippets of Erika's life, the guy's a controlling psycho."

Trevor stared at my phone for a long moment. "I agree."

"Is Erika still here?" I asked.

"Yes. I was just about to cut her loose, though. I got what I needed and now I have to think about it and try to put some evidence together."

"Do you think she could've done it?" I asked.

Trevor crossed his arms over his chest and shook his head. "Dang it, Gina. Before I saw that video of her expertly wielding a pink hammer, I was pretty sure she was innocent. Now... now, I have to put her back on the suspect list."

"Would she really leave that video up if she had killed Molly?" I asked.

"Maybe she forgot it was there. I don't know."

"Gina, can we leave now?" Daisy asked. "Pretty please? I've been such a good dog this whole time! And my nose is a super sniffer, so I smell things you can't. It stinks so bad in this building!"

"I don't think Erika did it," I said, patting her head and hoping it sufficed. "I don't have any evidence to back up that statement... in fact, this video shows the contrary. But her boyfriend? Now that's a different story."

"Most women don't kill in such a bloody fashion, either," Trevor muttered. "They prefer to keep their hands clean and use poison."

"Not *all* women," I said.

"Of course not. But a great deal of them would prefer to kill someone in a neat and tidy way instead of a bloodbath."

"But Nick... it sounds like he's got an anger problem. He's quite overprotective of Erika and borders on being a possessive jerk."

"I don't know, Gina." Trevor shook his head and pointed at my phone. "I personally think he crossed that line."

"Yeah, I agree."

We both stared at the device.

"Gina? Can you hear me?" Daisy asked. "You've been ignoring me. Can you still hear me speaking to you?"

"Yes."

"Yes what?" Trevor asked.

"Y-yes. I think you're right. Nick did cross the line into being a possessive jerk."

He furrowed his brow and stared at me a long while. "We just had that discussion."

"I need to get back to File It Away," I said, standing and hoping to put an end to the conversation. "I have clients coming in. I have to do my job, not yours."

"Yay!" Daisy shouted. "Get me out of this stinky place! My super sniffer needs a break!"

After pulling out his phone, he nodded. "Perfect timing. I'm going to be talking to Lewis Burton in a few minutes. I should be back just as he arrives."

"As in Lewis Burton, Molly's husband?"

He nodded.

I should just walk out, go about my business, and forget about the tragic killing, but curiosity kept rearing its head. I'd love to be a fly on the wall during the conversation *and* doing my clients' nails all at the same time. But cloning machines didn't exist at the local grocery store, so I'd have to settle with earning some money.

"Do you want to stop by later and tell me about it?" I asked.

"I can do that. But I thought you didn't want to be involved."

"I don't," I replied as we exited the room. "But maybe if you share your conversation with Lewis with me, something will stand out to me and you'll find he's the killer. A second set of ears, so to speak."

"But you aren't getting involved," Trevor replied, grinning.

"Nope. Just trying to help out if I can."

"Gina, you're a really bad liar," Daisy said, giggling. "I can totally tell you want to be involved in finding the murderer, and I'm just a talking dog!"

CHAPTER 4

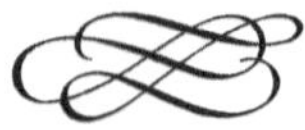

OKAY, so Daisy wasn't wrong. My intentions of minding my own business had been replaced by curiosity I would fight to slake.

Trevor dropped Daisy and me off at my store. My mind churned as I opened the door and took off my coat. I hoped Erika's boyfriend, Nick, didn't have anything to do with Molly's murder, but I sure did like him for it. Hopefully the evidence would be solid —maybe some fingerprints on the hammer and hopefully cameras that caught the whole thing.

"Yay!" Daisy yelled as I unleashed her. "It's time for my nap!" She trotted over to the bed in the corner of the store, curled up and closed her eyes. Moments later, she began to snore.

"Gina!" I turned as the door chimed to find my friend Annabelle sauntering in wearing a neon pink floor length parka and black and pink checkered boots. Heavy sparkly blue eyeliner and blue mascara framed her eyes. As the owner of Sage Advice, our local herbal apothecary, she'd been quite busy this winter as the colds and flu made their rounds. With our town doctor now dead, more and more people were turning to her for relief, and she provided it with her handmade tinctures and herbal remedies. I hadn't seen her since New Year's.

"Hey, Annabelle," I greeted her. "What's up? Do you need your nails done?"

She glanced down at her hands. "No, I don't think so. I just wanted to stop by and see if you wanted to go grab a coffee at Cup of Go. I haven't seen in you in, like, forever."

"Well, hi," I said, smiling. "And I can't. I have a customer in a few minutes, but you're welcome to stay if you like."

"Who is it?" she asked.

"Adrienne."

Her face broke out into a large grin. "Perfect. She's always fun."

We both turned when the door chimes rang. Adrienne stepped in and pulled off her black snow hat and matching parka. Long red hair cascaded around her slim shoulders as she tossed her head from side to side. She reminded me of a woman in a shampoo commercial, except she had no idea how beautiful she was, and I really liked that about her.

She smiled and waved.

"Hey, Adrienne," I said, pointing at a chair. "Take a seat and I'll get the water going."

As she glided over, she pulled a bottle of wine from her oversized bag. "I brought you a late Christmas present, Gina. Sorry I couldn't bring it by earlier."

She and her husband owned the town wine shop, Never Quit Wining, and made all their own products. "Oh, wow." I took the bottle from her and saw it was a Merlot. "Thank you so much. You know I love your wine."

"You're most welcome!"

"I already got my bottle," Annabelle said as she sat down next to Adrienne. "And I put that baby to bed, then used the bottle as a vase for some dried herbs. It looks so pretty in my little work studio."

After setting the gift behind the counter, I attended to Adrienne's feet.

The chatter eventually moved from the holidays to current events.

"I heard there was a murder at Hammer and Nail Hardware," Adrienne said, lowering her voice. "The owner, Molly Burton, was killed."

Annabelle gasped, her eyes widening as her mouth formed a perfect O. "I didn't know this! Did you, Gina?"

I nodded. "Yes. I spoke to Trevor earlier and we discussed it."

"Why am I always the last to know?" Annabelle whined. "What happened?"

"I heard she was shot," Adrienne said.

My head jerked up. "Where did you hear that?"

"Someone came into the store and said it," Adrienne replied. "Were they wrong?"

"Yes. Totally wrong!"

"Well, then why don't you tell us what happened, Miss Know-It-All?" Annabelle said.

I rolled my eyes, then focused on Adrienne's feet again. "She wasn't shot. She was beaten to death with a hammer."

"Eww," the two said in unison.

"I know. It sounds pretty awful, but I think the police have a good idea of who did it."

"Did you see the crime scene?" Adrienne asked.

"No, but I'm fairly certain being beaten with a hammer leaves things pretty bloody."

"Was it her husband?" Annabelle asked. "Did he do it?"

I shook my head. "No. Probably an employee or said employee's boyfriend."

"Dang it!" Annabelle shouted. "I thought for sure it would be the husband since Lewis was having an affair."

Silence blanketed the room as I pushed the red brush back into the bottle. If I didn't take a break and soak in this new development, I'd have paint all over Adrienne's toes. "What? Lewis was having an affair?"

A slow smile parted Annabelle's lips. Obviously thrilled she knew something I didn't, she nodded. "You weren't aware of that?" she asked innocently.

"Tell us everything!" Adrienne squealed.

"Well, I was getting my hair permed at Cut and Dyed. Molly was there, and things were so quiet, which is like, totally unusual."

I nodded. The hair salon was a henhouse of gossip, even worse than my store. With my straight, blonde hair, I only needed a haircut about once a quarter. Annabelle visited more often to keep her 80s perm in tip-top condition.

"Anyway, Molly got her hair cut, then left. After she walked out the door, the place, like, exploded in gossip. And that's when I learned Lewis was having an affair."

"With who?" Adrienne asked. "Anyone we may know?"

"Debbie Williams," Annabelle replied. "She works as the accountant out at Diamond Ranch."

"Doesn't Vic work there?" Adrienne asked.

"Yep. He's their head horse trainer. I'll ask him about her and see what he has to say."

The people of Diamond Ranch bred and trained high end horses, which, unfortunately, all looked the same to me.

I unscrewed the nail polish and returned to painting Adrienne's toes. My phone buzzed in my back pocket, but I ignored it. I'd wait until my customer was gone before answering.

"And did everyone think Molly knew?" I asked.

Annabelle shrugged. "It was just a bunch of chatter. Some people were surprised, some weren't."

"How long had the affair been going on?"

"A few months," Annabelle replied. "Apparently, Debbie was trying to convince Lewis to leave Molly, but obviously, he hadn't yet."

I finished up Adrienne's toes and took a moment to admire my work. "Nicely done, if I do say so myself. Give them a couple of minutes before you put your boots back on just to be safe, okay?"

"That's fine," Adrienne said. "I've got time."

Turning back to Annabelle, I asked, "How long had Molly known about the affair?"

"That I don't know. Maybe she found out, and she and Lewis got into a big fight about it. Or maybe he asked her for a divorce, and she said no."

I considered what Erika had shared about Molly's new involvement with the store. Perhaps she had been figuring out how much she'd get when she finally asked Lewis for a divorce. Had he said no and beat her with a hammer to keep his secret safe?

Or... maybe Debbie had decided it was time to get Molly out of the way and take Lewis for herself.

"I'll have to pass along that little nugget of information to Trevor," I muttered. "He was going to interview Lewis today, so it'll be interesting to see if he mentioned the affair."

"I think you should try to solve this," Annabelle said while my phone rang again.

"Nah." I shook my head. "I'm done with that."

Daisy trotted over and rested her head on my lap. "You're a liar, Gina. I know you want to find the killer."

"How's Daisy today?" Annabelle asked in what I liked to call her dog voice. It wasn't baby talk, but something a little deeper and she said her words weird. My dog loved it.

"I'm good, thank you." Daisy sighed, then wagged her tail as she approached Annabelle. "I spent the morning in the police station and all the bad smells made me tired and cranky. It was awful. I need to be petted."

"She's good," I said, smiling while Annabelle ran her hand over Daisy's head. The drama with that one was thick. "A bit worn out from our trip to the police station this morning, but she's fine."

"Why were you at the police station?" Adrienne asked.

"Trevor asked me to go down and talk to one of the suspects. For some reason, she said she'd only speak to me. So, as a favor to my friend, I had a little chat with her at the station."

"Why would she only speak to you?" Annabelle asked. "And who was it?"

"Erika Roscoe. She worked as a cashier at Hammer and Nail."

"Is she the one with the TikTok channel?" Adrienne asked.

My gaze widened in surprise. "Yes! Do you watch her?"

"I do. She's saved us so much money in repairs around the store. With these buildings being so old, it seems there's always something broken. I've learned a lot from her."

For some reason, I hadn't thought Erika had much of a following. Later, I'd check into her account once again. The number of followers had probably been staring me right in the face and I hadn't noticed it.

"Why would she only talk to you?" Annabelle repeated. "And why is she a person of interest to the sheriff's department?"

"Trevor had heard that she and Molly had a disagreement the night she was killed, so he wanted to talk to her about it. But she said she would only speak with me because she didn't trust the police. She begged me to find the killer."

I didn't share the videos I'd found by scrolling through her TikTok channel. Word that she'd been at the sheriff's department was certain to spread, and I didn't want to add to the gossip by mentioning the damning evidence.

"That seems weird," Annabelle muttered. "I mean, they just wanted to talk to her. I don't see what the big deal is."

"Mallory doesn't exactly have the best track record of finding murderers," Adrienne replied. "I get why she'd be nervous. I would be if I were in her shoes."

"Well, thankfully, Mallory is out of town and Trevor's in charge. I'm sure he'll run a proper investigation," I said, standing. My phone buzzed again and I pulled it out. My second client had canceled, claiming the snow was too heavy on her road for her to get the car out. Hopefully, the plow had been down my road because I was in no mood to deal with a stuck car. I also had two missed phone calls from a rescue organization in Flagstaff. With a groan, I shoved the device back in my pocket. I didn't want to be called out for a dog rescue, especially in this weather. My bones already felt frozen and I was unable to get warm.

But the potential dog that needed my help... of course I'd go if I was summoned to do so.

Adrienne stuffed her feet into her boots, then glanced out the door. "I wish the snow would stop."

"I think everyone does." She handed me a credit card, and I ran the charge then gave it back to her. "Have a great day, Adrienne."

"Oh! I wanted to check that this is the same person you saw today." She pulled up her phone, scrolled for a moment, then faced it toward me. On the screen, Erika was showing her audience the difference between a spud wrench and a crescent wrench. "Yes, that's her."

I'd seen the video earlier. It had been located right below the one where she slammed the pink hammer into the wall. "Wait a minute." I grabbed Adrienne's phone and scrolled up and down as I searched for the thumbnail that I recalled from that video.

Nothing.

I even played a few just to make sure I hadn't lost my mind. The video was nowhere to be found.

Erika had deleted it.

If that didn't scream guilt, I wasn't sure what did.

50

CHAPTER 5

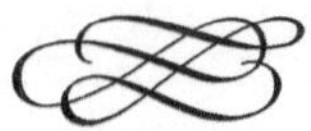

I FOLLOWED the snowplow the whole way home while snowflakes continued to fall. A winter like this hadn't been seen in ages.

Once inside, I poured myself a glass of the wine Adrienne had given me, then settled on my sofa with a blanket, Daisy, and flames dancing in the fireplace.

Then, I called the Flagstaff rescue.

"Hi, Corey," I said. "It's Gina Dunner returning your call."

"Hey, Gina," he replied. "Did you have a nice holiday season?"

We chatted about family being in town, Christmas presents received, and the New Year's party he attended. Unfortunately, I didn't have a great story to share about that night. I'd been asleep by eight. He lightly chided me about my old lady ways, but then he got down to business. "I've got two dogs that are bonded like I can't believe. I was wondering if you could foster them for a bit while I head out of town."

As my shoulder sagged in relief, I said, "Sure. How long?" No freezing cold rescue mission for me.

"Just two weeks."

"Do you want me to see if I can have them adopted?"

"That would be fine, but they can't be separated. Someone has to take both of them."

"Wow. Are they really that close?"

"They won't go outside without each other. I've never seen them in different rooms. I had to take one to the vet and he wouldn't leave without the other."

"Okay. We can work around all that. What are their names? Where did they come from?"

"Frank and Marilyn."

"Those are odd dog names."

"Yeah, I know. Apparently, their owner, who passed away, loved Frank Sinatra and Marilyn Monroe."

"Aww... that's sweet."

"I thought so, too."

"When did you want to drop them by?"

"Does tomorrow work? I can swing over on my way to Utah. My aunt's sick, so my mom wants me to come home for a bit."

I furrowed my brow. "Sorry to hear that, Corey. Is it serious?"

"We don't know. Mom just suggested that I come home, and even though I'm almost thirty, I still do exactly what she tells me. I think I may need therapy."

I laughed again. "No, you're being smart. Moms know everything. If she says to come home, you do it."

My mood suddenly soured. So far, I'd done a stellar job ignoring the dark family secrets my father had told me before the holidays, which had consisted of him being the kingpin drug dealer of Arizona and a turf war which had threatened my mother's life. She'd disappeared and no one knew if she was dead or alive. Trevor had offered to look into it for me, and I'd accepted his help. However, I'd also ordered him not to share his findings until I asked.

I hadn't.

"Bring them by tomorrow afternoon," I said. "I'll see you then."

I hung up and stared at the phone on my lap for a long while, doing my best not to confront my thoughts about my mother, my father, or my past. The wine and fire had made me sleepy. Just as I laid my head back to rest for a bit while listening to Daisy's soft snores, someone knocked on the door.

Daisy flew from the couch, barking incessantly, which translated to a bunch of gibberish. She always barked when suddenly woken from a nap and she never had anything coherent to say about it. Taking a deep breath, I calmed my racing heart, then begrudgingly flipped the blanket back to answer the door.

"Hey!" Trevor greeted me.

"Gina! It's Trevor!" Daisy yelled as she jumped up and down. "I love Trevor! Pet me! Pet me! Did you see how good I was at your stinky workplace today?"

"Come in," I grumbled as I opened the

screen door and a blast of cold air hit me in the face. "I've got a fire going and a bottle of wine open."

"It's three in the afternoon," Trevor said, shutting the door and turning the deadbolt.

"Yes, but it's five o'clock somewhere. Will you be joining me?"

"Sure. I'm off work now, so I might as well."

I fetched a wine glass from the kitchen then returned to the living room. Trevor had sat down on the end of my couch while Daisy had stretched out from one end to the other, her head on his lap. His uniform would be covered in dog hair if he allowed her to stay so close, but I said nothing. A little dog hair never hurt anyone.

I returned to my side of the sofa, wiggled under the blanket so I didn't disturb my dog, and poured him a glass.

"Cheers," he said as we clinked glasses.

"Cheers. What happened with Lewis?" I'd decided to keep everything I'd learned during my gossip session to myself for now. Of course, I'd share it with Trevor, but I wanted to hear what he had to say first.

He took a long sip of wine. "This is good. Is it from Never Quit Wining?"

I nodded. "Adrienne brought it to me today."

He drank again, then set the glass down. "Well, my chat with Lewis was... interesting."

"How so?"

"He was furious Molly fired Erika. He said she was one of his best employees."

"Did he know about the TikTok videos?"

Trevor nodded. "He did. Thought they were cute. He didn't mind that she used the store at all and thought it was a load of B.S. that Molly was suddenly angry about it. He seemed to be really fond of Erika, in an almost paternal way."

Was it creepy or nice for an employer to feel fatherly about an employee? I wasn't sure. "Why was Molly suddenly interested in the store?" I asked.

"Lewis thought it was because she was going to divorce him."

"Why would she do that?"

"Because she was having an affair." Trevor picked up his wine glass and drank. "He'd only found out about it recently, but he seemed pretty broken up about it."

I realized the Burton marriage was one of complete dysfunction, lies and secrets.

"Who's the guy?" I asked.

"Bryce Willis. Do you know him?"

I shook my head. Even though Heywood was a small town, I pretty much kept to myself. Socializing wasn't my forte, but now that my son was at college, I should probably get out more. Otherwise, I'd end up the cranky old lady hiding in her house with a pack of dogs.

But was that such a bad thing?

"I don't, either. From what I understand, he lives in the trailer park just outside of town and works at the recycling plant in between here and Sedona."

"How did he find out about her affair?"

"She was reading a text message Bryce sent her and didn't hear Lewis come into the room. He came up behind her to give her a kiss on the neck and got a proverbial slap in the face instead."

I winced and took a sip of wine. "Ouch."

"She swore she was ending it," Trevor

continued. "But Lewis had been snooping around in her email and phone, and found out she hadn't. He seemed pretty broken-hearted about it."

"Was he brokenhearted enough to kill her?"

Trevor chuckled and shook his head. "That I don't know."

"Where was he last night?"

"He said he left the store shortly after Erika was fired and he didn't go back. He went home and got drunk, then passed out. When he woke in the morning, he realized Molly hadn't come home, so he rushed back to the store and found her dead."

"Did you believe him?" I asked, recalling Erika had mentioned she thought she saw a man standing in the shadows at the end of the hallway when she confronted Molly.

Trevor sighed, then nodded. "I did. There wasn't anything he said that set off my radar."

I stared at my empty wine glass, my thoughts swirling. "Why didn't he stop Molly from firing Erika?"

"Because he was trying to keep the peace. Things had been tough for him as he tried to come to terms with his wife's infidelity, and he was wondering if she was going to try to take him for all he had financially. He felt that if there was a bigger fight about Erika than they already had, then it could be used against him during the divorce... maybe Molly claiming verbal abuse or something."

"It sounds like he could've done it," I muttered. "Especially if he was worried about her fleecing him."

"I don't know, Gina. In the marriage, it sounds like he got shafted. He was pretty upset about Molly's murder."

"Was he upset enough to call his girlfriend?"

Trevor began to cough as wine shot out his nose.

I winced. "Ouch. I'm sorry. I bet that hurt."

He hurried from the couch into the kitchen as Daisy jumped down and began sniffing the discarded wine that had landed on the coffee table. At least he'd missed my carpet.

"Please don't lick that up," I whispered. "It came out of his nose."

She glanced up at me, then back to the mess. "Okay," she said, returning to the couch. After circling three times, she lay down again.

As Trevor continued to cough and sputter in the kitchen, I gently caressed Daisy, hoping she'd get along okay with the bonded pair I had arriving the next day. Should I tell her or not? Either way, she may become anxious. Bringing new dogs together was always tricky. Sometimes they gelled effortlessly; other times, they didn't get along. It was no different than humans meeting each other for the first time—except for the rear end sniffing.

Trevor returned, sat down and used a napkin from the kitchen to wipe up the discarded wine from his nose. He glanced over at me and shook his head.

"I'm sorry about that," I apologized again. "It was horrible timing to drop that bomb on you."

"No kidding. Pass me that bottle, please."

After I shoved it across the table, he poured another glass, drank a few gulps, then set it down and turned to me. "Now, please share the details, Gina. This will be interesting."

I smiled at the way the corner of his lip lifted when he was annoyed with me, almost as if he snarled. "I should've told you when you first walked in. But yes, Lewis is not the innocent one. He's just as guilty as Molly."

As I shared my conversation with Adrienne and Annabelle, he stared at me. Slowly, his lip began to relax. When I finished, he chuckled. "I had no idea. He really seemed broken up about losing his wife, even if they had fought that night."

"His mistress, Debbie Williams, works as an accountant out at Diamond Ranch."

"Wow. You sure got a lot of good information. I bet Vic knows her."

"Probably. And that's why I'm going to see him tomorrow. You're welcome to join me if you'd like."

"Confronting Lewis' mistress about Molly's murder? I wouldn't miss that for the world."

CHAPTER 6

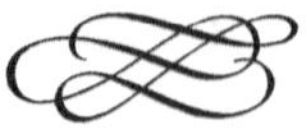

I woke early the next morning, and it took everything I had to leave my cozy electric blanket. After a quick shower, I forced Daisy outside. Even though she whined the whole time, my mood remained high simply because we hadn't received anymore snow overnight. The drive out to Diamond Ranch should be easy.

As I pulled out a couple of blankets and draped them over the dog beds in my room, Daisy studied me with a critical eye. "Who is coming to stay with us?" she asked.

"What do you mean?"

"You know exactly what I mean, Gina. I can tell you're getting ready for more dogs."

I nodded and decided to let her in on everything. "We have two coming to stay with us. They'll be here this afternoon, and their names are Frank and Marilyn."

"That doesn't sound like dog names."

"No, you're right."

"That sounds like they're hoity-toity, snooty dogs."

"I'm sure they're perfectly nice," I said. "We just need to be welcoming to them."

"How long are they going to be here?"

"Two weeks, unless we can get them adopted."

"Maybe they'll want to play with me and be my friends. Not like that Zeus who wanted to eat me."

"He didn't want to eat you, Daisy," I said, rolling my eyes. "He just had some... issues."

As a super high energy dog, he'd been destructive and an absolute jerk, but he was the Sedona fire department's problem now. Last I heard, Zeus was doing wonderfully in his new home and was passing training with flying colors.

"He had so, so many issues." She sat down and stared at me as I arranged the last blanket. "He was a very bad dog, Gina. I hope these two are good dogs, like me."

"We'll find out this afternoon," I said. When a knock sounded at the front door, Daisy spun around and ran down the hall barking.

"It's Trevor," I called. "Not a serial killer."

Well, at least I hoped not.

I opened the door and smiled. "Come on in. I just need to finish up in the bedroom, grab my coat and I'll be ready."

"Hi, Daisy," he said, leaning down to give her a rub behind her ears. "How are you today?"

"I'm good, Trevor! So good! We have more dogs coming today, Trevor! I hope they'll play with me and be my new best friends!"

It was always amusing watching Daisy speak with people who couldn't hear her. Trevor grinned and continued to pet her as she prattled on about her new friends arriving.

I left the two in the front hall and hurried back to the bedroom. After glancing around to make sure I'd put away my shoes and slippers so the new dogs wouldn't be tempted to chew on them, I also closed the bathroom door and the dresser drawers. The dogs deserved a chance at showing me their good behavior, so I made it easy by closing off anywhere that would tempt them to get in trouble.

While walking down the hall, I also shut the door to my son, Jacob's, room and took a glance around the kitchen. Everything was put away. The living room couch still held my blanket, but I could fold that later.

"Okay, let's go," I said, slipping on my coat. "What time do you need to be back at the office?"

"Noon."

"Perfect. We shouldn't be there long."

Daisy pouted as we stepped outside and I locked the door.

"I hate you for leaving me!" she yelled. "I hate you so much, Gina! I'm going to sit here and think of ways to get back at you!"

Before guilt changed my mind, I swore and hurried toward Trevor's truck. That dog had me wrapped around her paws and knew exactly what buttons to push to get me to do what she wanted.

The two-lane highway leading out to Diamond Ranch was sandwiched between tall pine trees, their branches heavy with sun-drenched sparkling snow. Even though I'd lived in Heywood my whole life, I never ceased to be amazed at the beauty nature had bestowed on the area.

As Trevor pulled off the freeway and onto the dirt road, I noted the snow had been scraped down nicely, allowing us to pass without problem.

"Oh, no," I muttered as we reached the circular driveway.

"What?" Trevor asked.

I pointed at the boot lodged upside down onto the fence post. "Vic told me that means the farm has lost a horse."

Trevor slowed as we drove past it. "I had no idea. I've seen that on other farms in the area as well."

"Yeah," I sighed. "It's a tribute to the horse. Since the boot isn't covered in snow, I'm assuming it happened recently."

"That's too bad."

We pulled up in front of the big house and I took a deep breath before opening the car door. Never had I been to Diamond Ranch on good terms. The first time, I'd spilled wine all over the owner's white dress and her matching carpet. Another time, I'd been attempting to get Vic out of there when he'd been accused of murdering his ex-girlfriend, Phoebe. I'd also been on the property spying on some potential suspects, and finally, I'd been drugged and tied up in a barn, then discovered that the former owner, Roger Wagner, had killed Phoebe.

"You okay?" Trevor asked, furrowing his brow.

"Yeah. Just a lot of negative history between me and this place."

"There sure is," he replied. He took my hand in his. "Do you want to wait in the car?"

I stared at his fingers over mine and found the gesture comforting. "Nope. I'm all in on this visit."

As we moved through the mud and snow to the side door of the big house, I was happy I'd worn my old boots. Vic had told me the offices were on the west side of the building, while Mrs. Wagner lived in the main part of the house and oversaw the ranch since her now ex-husband was doing time in prison for murder.

Trevor was about to tap on the door, but then we heard someone call my name. Both of us turned to find Vic walking our way. Wearing a black hat, matching jeans and cowboy boots and a black and white checkered flannel coat, he gave off all sorts of "bad" cowboy vibes. Thankfully, that was no longer true. After Phoebe's death, he'd resolved to clean up his life, and so far, he'd been successful. I smiled as the big lug approached.

"How's my little runt of a sister?" he asked as he scooped me up into a big bear hug and rubbed his beard on my cheek, something he knew I hated, but often did anyway.

"I'm fine," I growled, pushing his face away from mine. Somehow, I'd lost the height gene pool lottery. While my brother stood over six feet, I was five-foot-three on a good day. He set me down and turned to Trevor. As they shook hands, they had a quick discussion about the last football game the Cardinals had blown while I gently rubbed the side of my face and hoped I didn't have a beard burn. If I did, I'd have to sneak back and flush some socks down his toilet to clog it.

"Are you two here to talk to Debbie?" Vic asked.

Trevor nodded. "Gina brought me some interesting information. Apparently, Debbie and Lewis Griffin are having an affair."

"That's what she told me when she called yesterday." He actually reached over and mussed my hair, as if I were a child. "That's what Gina does. Pokes her nose where it doesn't belong."

"I recall you begging me to do exactly that so you wouldn't go to prison," I said. "Remember that?"

"Yeah, I do," Vic sighed, his smile fading. "But we're family, Gina. I hate to see you putting yourself in danger for no reason."

Family. Sometimes, when he and my father threw around that term with such weight, I felt like I was a member of the mafia. Just change my last name to Corleone. And maybe in a way, I was a member, even though

I'd only recently found out about my family's sordid history.

"I'm not putting myself in danger," I replied. "I'm here to talk to an accountant. How threatening can that be?"

"You haven't met Debbie," Vic said. "She's vicious." He gave me a wink, then knocked on the door. "Hey, Debbie! Open up!"

A long moment passed and just as I was about to ask Vic for his definition of "vicious," the door swung open.

"What are you out here screaming about?" I studied the woman before me. Maybe a few years older than me, her deep elevens between her eyebrows gave her a perpetual frown, even when she smiled as she saw Vic. Odd. The top part of her face looked angry while she grinned. "Vic! What do you want now?"

Vic smiled and tilted his head to the side. "I came by to introduce my sister to the prettiest accountant I know."

I rolled my eyes and made a gagging sound while Trevor glared at me. Not that

Debbie was unattractive, but my brother's attempt at manipulation was.

Thankfully, Debbie hadn't noticed my antics and she batted her eyelashes at him. "You're so sweet." Turning to me, she stuck out her hand. "You must be this darling's sister. I'm Debbie."

"Gina Dunner," I said, taking her palm in mine. "It's nice to meet you."

"And you as well. Any relative of Vic's is a friend of mine." She turned to Trevor. "Who is this?"

"Trevor Hutchison," he replied with a grin. "It's really nice to meet you."

They shook hands, and then she motioned us all inside. "Come, come. It's so dang cold."

I could agree with that.

We followed her into the small space containing a desk, and two guest chairs. A computer sat to her right while a pile of receipts had been piled to her left. She took a seat behind the desk and folded her hands on the surface. It was then that I noticed scratches on her forearms. Quickly, I sat in a chair so I could study them closer. Trevor took the seat next to me while I felt Vic's presence behind me. There wasn't anywhere else for him to go.

"What can I do for you?" she asked, her smile still firmly in place, along with her furrowed brow.

Trevor leaned forward and placed his elbows on his knees. "I'm with the Sheriff's department, Debbie. I'm looking into the death of Molly Burton."

Her grin faded a bit as she shot a glare at Vic. "I didn't know you were police."

"Sorry I didn't mention that," Trevor replied. "Did you know Molly?"

As her face paled, she studied her desk, then slowly pulled down her sleeves to hide the scratches. "I didn't."

"So you didn't know she was murdered?" Trevor asked.

The woman slowly shook her head.

"This is a delicate subject, but word around town is that you're having an affair with her husband."

An anvil of silence slammed over the room. I feared people would hear my breathing, so I held it.

When Debbie slowly raised her head, the

smile was gone. Instead, her mouth had formed a hard, fine line, her eyes blazing with fury. "Word around town?" she hissed. "You've got to be kidding me." She stood up so fast, her chair fell backward. "What kind of cop are you? You're here because of *gossip*?"

Trevor smiled. "A simple yes or no would be fine, ma'am. We don't need the outrage."

Her nostrils flared as her hands fisted at her sides.

"A woman is dead. You live in Heywood. People gossip here, Debbie," Trevor continued. "If you just answer the question, I can be out of your hair."

Her cheeks turned cherry-red. If she flew over the desk and attempted to gouge out his eyes, I wouldn't have been surprised.

Trevor stood and placed his hands on his hips. "And if you don't answer my questions here, then we can head down to the station."

Apparently, the idea of going down to the Sheriff's Department deflated her bluster. She sat down and placed her elbows on the desk, her head in her hands. Her actions spoke louder than any words. If she tried to deny the affair, she'd be lying.

"Yes," she whispered. "Lewis and I were having an affair."

"You *were* having an affair, or you *are*?" I asked.

With a glare, she spat, "I don't know. I haven't heard from him since Molly died."

"So you *did* know she died," I pointed out.

She nodded slowly.

I didn't expect Lewis to run into the arms of his lover after his wife had been killed, but I would think he may have at least given her a call. Phone records would have to be studied.

"Have you tried to contact him?" I asked.

She nodded. "Many times, but he hasn't returned my calls."

"Can you tell us where you were the night Molly was killed?" Trevor asked.

"I was at home. *Alone.*"

"No one saw you?" Trevor asked. "Did you have any food delivered? Maybe talk to someone on the phone?"

She shook her head. "Lewis was supposed to come over, but he never did."

"How close are the two of you?" I asked.

Tears welled in her eyes. "I love that man

with every fiber of my being. I've been asking him to leave Molly for weeks now. I wanted us to have a chance at a life together, and he said he did, too."

Had Debbie wanted a life with Lewis so badly that she'd killed his wife?

CHAPTER 7

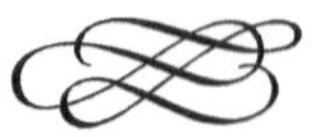

"Thanks for your time," Trevor said. "If I have any further questions, I'd really like to stop by again, if that's okay."

Debbie swiped at her tears. "That's fine. I'm not going anywhere, and I have nothing to hide."

I followed Trevor out of the office while Vic stayed inside for a moment. I heard him trying to cheer up Debbie as I shut the door behind me.

"What do you think?" Trevor asked.

"She's hiding something," I replied softly. "Did you see her arms?"

He furrowed his brow. "No. What's up with the arms?"

"She's got a bunch of scratches on her forearms." I ran my hand over my coat where I'd seen the marks. "Like she'd been in a fight or something."

He stared at me a long moment, then opened the door. "Hey, Debbie? Can you tell me where you got those scratches on your arms?"

"Can you just leave her alone?" Vic asked. "She's really upset."

Trevor shrugged. "I just need to know about the scratches, then I'm on my way."

"My cat!" Debbie shrieked. "I have a new kitten who's a psychopath!"

As she wailed and swore, Trevor shut the door. "She's really angry."

"If I were in her shoes, I would be too, but the questions need to be asked."

We stood in silence, waiting for Vic. He stepped out just as my teeth began to chatter.

"She's not going to cooperate with you guys any longer," Vic said. "She's furious that you're asking questions about her relationship with Lewis, as well as where she was the night Molly died."

"You need to check her phone records," I

said, pointing at Trevor. "I think she's lying through her teeth. If I had to put money on it right now, I'd say Lewis and Debbie are in on this together. They're waiting for it all to blow over."

Trevor pulled out his phone and tapped on the screen. I assumed it was a note to himself to check the records as I'd suggested.

"Also see if she really has a cat," I said. "I don't believe a word she said in there."

"Are you the one running this investigation, or am I?" Trevor asked, smiling.

"Sorry. I just hate liars." I pulled out my own phone and glanced at the time. "I need to get back."

"What do you have going on?" Vic asked.

"Two new dogs. A rescuer from Sedona is dropping them off. I'm hoping they're well-mannered and nothing like the last guy, Zeus."

"Good," Vic replied. "I want you busy and to stay out of this investigation."

I sighed and rolled my eyes. "Who are you, my mother?"

A heavy silence fell around us. Our

mother hadn't been around to tell us to do anything.

"Okay, that was a bad choice of words," I admitted. "But mind your own business, Vic. I'm an adult and I'll do exactly as I please."

"You're my little sister and I don't want to see you hurt," he said.

"The caveat being it's okay for me to stick my nose into a murder investigation as long as you're the main suspect."

"Okay," Trevor interrupted. "I'll be taking you home now, Gina. Vic, it was good to see you, and I'm sorry about the loss of the horse." He gestured toward the boot on the fence.

Vic glanced over his shoulder. "Yeah, that was a tough one to take. Her name was Grace Jones and one of the finest mares we had. Besides being a really sweet horse, she gave us some beautiful foals."

"That's too bad," I said, studying my brother's face carefully. He loved the horses with every fiber of his being, and like me, he'd do anything to help an animal. When his eyes welled with tears, he quickly swiped them away.

"I'll see you two later," he said, not meeting my gaze. "Mind your own business, Gina."

Trevor and I returned to the truck as Vic hurried into the heart of the farm.

On the way back to my house, I considered whether I should contact the author who hired me as a ghostwriter. I'd completed two mystery novels for her, and she'd been thrilled with both. However, I'd been involved in those investigations and was able to apply my real-life experiences to the book. If I was to write a third for her, that would mean I'd have to dive into Molly's murder. Currently, I was participating, but it hadn't consumed me as the other two had.

I'd have to think on whether to contact her or not. First, I'd have to see how the rescue dogs reacted to their new surroundings. If there was going to be problems, I needed to stick pretty close to the house for the next couple of weeks. Besides, for all I knew, Debbie had offed Molly in a fit of jealous rage over Lewis and Trevor would have everything wrapped up by this afternoon.

"Thanks for coming with me," Trevor said as he pulled into my driveway. "I hadn't noticed the scratches on her arms. It was good you were there."

"You're welcome," I replied. "Let me know what happens."

"I was going to go have a chat with Bryce Willis, Molly's side piece. Did you want to go with me?"

I practically jumped at the idea, but remembered the dogs, not to mention me questioning if I really did want to be involved. And then there were my brother's warnings…

"Let me get back to you on that," I said. "If I don't go, I hope you'll tell me everything that was said."

"Sure. It always seems to help to run things by you about the investigation. I think you called it, 'a second set of ears.' I'll call you later."

I waved as he backed out onto the main street, then turned to the front door. Daisy barked as I slid the key in the lock.

"Gina! Gina!" she yelled once I stepped inside. "I was wondering if you'd ever come home! You were gone for so long! I missed you *so* much! "

I leaned over and pet her, glad she was happy to see me. She hadn't been when I left. "I was gone two hours, Daisy. That's it. And, I don't know how many times I have to tell you this, but I will always come back for you. Always."

"Are you sure that's all the time you were gone?" she asked as she rolled onto her back. "It seemed like years. Decades even."

I gave her belly a quick rub, then shucked my coat and hung it. My stomach grumbled from not eating yet, so I hurried into the kitchen. After opening the refrigerator door, I stared at the sparse offerings. When my son, Jacob, had been living at home, I always kept my refrigerator stocked. Now, being on my own, I survived on cottage cheese and turkey sandwiches.

And I was out of turkey.

"Cottage cheese it is," I mumbled. I grabbed the container and pulled down my glasses to study the expiration date, which was two days ago. I was playing with fire, but my hunger pains won out.

I ate quickly and finished up just as my phone buzzed. Corey was alerting me he was in the driveway.

"Daisy, I need you to go to the bedroom," I called. "The new dogs are here and I want them to sniff around before they meet you."

"You want me to be locked away in my own house?" She trotted into the kitchen and sat down, glaring at me. "Who exactly is in charge here? Them or you?"

"Fine," I huffed. "Just don't cause any trouble, okay?"

"I'm a good dog, Gina. I don't cause trouble."

A half-dozen instances came to mind when she hadn't been a good dog. The time I caught her with my slipper in her mouth but she swore she wasn't chewing on it, or when I found her in the kitchen with the trash can on its side, but of course, she wasn't responsible for it. And then there was the time I opened the front door and she chased a cat for three blocks until it turned and attacked her, sending her scampering back home. However, I decided not to voice them.

Corey lightly tapped on the door, and I smiled as I opened it.

Tall and thin with a mop of brown hair and a long, pointy nose, he was a sweet kid. Well, he was in his late twenties, but he was still a kid to me.

"Hey, Gina," he said shyly as his cheeks turned pink.

"Hi, Corey." I glanced down at the two dogs. The small, brown one looked like a dachshund, the other was brown and black, some sort of shepherd mix, with heavy emphasis on German Shepherd. "Hi, guys," I said in a quiet voice. "Welcome."

Daisy peeked around my legs, her tail slapping against the base of the entry way table.

"Come on in," I said. "It's freezing out there."

"Very true," Corey replied. He stepped inside and closed the door firmly behind him. Daisy and the two dogs sniffed each other.

"My name's Daisy!" she shouted. "We can be friends and we can all play and run around! It's going to be so much fun!"

She took off into the living room, jumped

on the couch, spun around in a circle, then returned to the entry way.

"Okay, let's calm down," I ordered. "Give them a chance to get used to the house, Daisy."

"Do you want me to unleash them?" Corey asked.

I nodded then grabbed Daisy's collar to keep her in place.

After unclipping their leashes, the two dogs slowly sniffed around the living room. The shepherd led the way, with the little dachshund trailing close behind.

"The big one is Marilyn, and the little guy is Frank," Corey said. "He's very protective of his girl."

I chuckled as the two moved to the kitchen. Frank had to take four steps to every one of Marilyn's to keep up.

"They never want to be apart," Corey continued. "They won't even sleep in separate beds."

"They're an interesting pair," I said. Frank followed Marilyn around as if he were her bodyguard.

"I think they'd be best in a quiet house,"

Corey said. "They're both really content with hanging out on the couch all day. They could even go to someone who works long hours as long as the house has a doggy-door. They both like people and I've never seen either one act aggressive toward a human, but they prefer each other's company."

"Good to know."

Daisy squirmed, trying to wrench out of my grasp. "I want to go play!" she yelled. "They're going to be my new friends!"

"What about other dogs?" I asked. "How do they do with other dogs?"

Corey shrugged. "I've never had a problem with that. I've got five other rescues I'm fostering right now, and these two just keep to themselves."

"And you said they don't have behavioral issues, right?"

"None. Frank and Marilyn are very well-behaved, as long as they're together."

I released Daisy's collar and she ran over to them. "Hi! Hi!" she said, her tail moving so fast, it became a white and brown streak. "I'm Daisy! We can be friends!"

Frank moved in between her and Marilyn,

lifted his lip and sat down. Daisy's tail slowly came to a halt and she took a few steps back.

"Well, I guess I'll head to my mom's now," Corey said. "I really appreciate you watching them, Gina. Send me a text and let me know how they're doing."

"Of course. Drive safely."

After he left, I turned back to the dogs. Daisy now cowered in a corner of the couch while Frank and Marilyn stared at her.

"What's wrong?" I asked.

"They don't want to be my friends," Daisy pouted. "They told me to leave them alone."

If dogs could cry, mine would be sobbing. "It's okay. They just need time to get used to you."

I sat down on the couch and stroked her head.

"Frank said that I'm not allowed near Marilyn unless he says so, and he told me he doesn't like me."

I glanced over at my two new charges. "He's going to have to learn that's not the way things work in this house."

Frank stared back at me, then turned to

Marilyn. Both curled up against each other in the corner of the living room, obviously not interested in me or Daisy.

"See, Gina?" she said. "They're being mean to me. I'm not sure who is worse: that big, dumb blond, Zeus, or these two. At least Zeus wanted to play a lot."

"I'm sorry, Daisy," I muttered.

As Frank bared his teeth at Daisy once again, I wondered how I was going to keep the peace in my house until the dogs were either adopted, or Corey returned.

CHAPTER 8

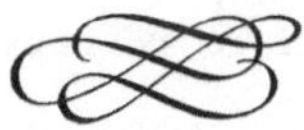

By the next morning, it became apparent things would be smooth sailing with my two guests, as long as Daisy didn't bother them. Despite her encouraging them to join us in the bedroom at bedtime, they had slept in the living room, which had only hurt Daisy's feelings more. I felt bad for my little brown and white extrovert, but the situation also allowed me to focus on other things. Namely, who killed Molly Burton.

Although initially I hadn't wanted to get involved, the case was now consuming me and it was all I could think about. I decided to send an email to the author who hired me as a ghostwriter and tell her I had another murder mystery for her if she wanted it. If I couldn't figure out who killed Molly, I'd just have to fabricate some of the details and the ending, like I'd done with other genres I'd written. I'd never been on a spaceship before, but I'd written a space romance, and it had turned out quite well. Besides, I did have access to the Sheriff's department. Trevor seemed fine allowing me to tag along while he talked to people, and it also appeared he appreciated my input on the case.

As I poured my second cup of coffee, I heard growling from the living room. I found Daisy and Frank in a standoff, with Marilyn behind her protector, watching.

"Daisy, just let them be!" I pleaded. "They don't want to play, they don't want to be friends!"

"I think Marilyn does," Daisy replied. "Except I have to get past this little tyrant. He should've been named Napoleon."

Furrowing my brow, I asked, "How do you know about Napoleon?"

"Jacob had to do a paper on him, so I watched a documentary with him. This little brown turd reminds me of him. I can take him, Gina. I'll win a fight."

"Daisy, there will not be any fighting in my house," I ordered. After grabbing her collar, I dragged her into the kitchen with me. "Why do you need to press this?"

"Because I think Marilyn is being held against her will!"

I rolled my eyes. "Did she tell you that, or did your imagination?"

"No one did," she muttered, curling up under the table. "It's just a feeling I have."

"Have you asked her?"

"No. She won't talk to me."

I glanced back into the living room. Frank licked the side of Marilyn's face and she closed her eyes, relaxed. They were very cute together, and Marilyn didn't seem like the hostage Daisy thought she was.

In order to leave the two lovebirds at peace, Daisy would have to accompany me everywhere I went. Not that she would mind. She was always up for an adventure, even if that meant a simple trip to the grocery store.

My phone call to Trevor went directly to voicemail, where I left a message that if he still wanted me to accompany him to see Bryce Willis, I could. Now that I'd decided I really wanted to figure out who killed Molly and the new dogs would be fine, I hope he didn't shut me out.

"I wonder if the hardware store is open again?" I asked my now sleeping dog. Since I had no idea how long it took to clear a crime scene, I texted Trevor, then stared at the phone waiting for a reply.

Of course, he was in the middle of a murder investigation and wasn't at my beck and call, but it still irritated me when he didn't immediately return my text.

Instead of vacuuming the house, throwing in a load of laundry and washing the dishes piling up in the sink, I decided to head over to Sage Advice and see Annabelle and her boyfriend, Doug. Then, on the way home, I could stop at the grocery store, and hopefully at some point I'd hear from Trevor.

"Come on, Daisy," I said. "Let's go see Jack."

"Yay!" She burst out from under the table. "I love Jack!"

Annabelle's beagle preferred to spend his

days chasing sunbeams to lie in, but he did like to play with Daisy when we visited.

I retrieved my jacket and Daisy's leash, then checked in on my two guests who were still joined at the hip while enjoying the blankets on the couch. "I need to go," I said. "You two be good, okay?"

Why I always talked to dogs as if they comprehended every word I said, I'd never understand. It didn't make logical sense, but I continued to do it. Except for Daisy, not one had ever spoken back to me.

"I'm leaving, too, losers," Daisy said, standing at my side. "So neener, neener, neener."

"Daisy, be nice," I scolded.

She didn't listen. "Only *bad* dogs have to stay at home. That's not me. I'm a *good* dog, unlike you two."

"Daisy!"

"Maybe when I get back I'll play with you... if you're lucky." With the final insult, she trotted over to the front door and stared at it, as if willing it to open. "Let's go, Gina!"

Should I correct her rude behavior or let it slide? I had no idea if Frank and Marilyn even understood her when she wasn't speaking dog. They both stared up at me. Frank sighed, and if he were able, I imagined he'd roll his eyes. I got the distinct impression they were waiting for me to leave.

I followed Daisy to the front door and we braved the frigid outdoors. Thankfully, the heater in the car revved up quickly, and by the time we'd hit Heywood proper, I was nice and toasty.

After finding a parking spot a few stores down from Sage Advice, I glanced at the people on the sidewalk. To my surprise, Debbie Williams hurried by.

"I wonder where she's going?" I asked Daisy.

"Who?"

"Debbie Williams."

"I don't know who that is."

Right. She'd stayed home while we visited the horse ranch.

"Let's go for a walk," I said, exiting the car.

"Yay! I love walks!"

I leashed her up and we followed Debbie.

After a few moments, Daisy said, "Gina, I

changed my mind. It's cold. I don't want to walk."

"Come on," I muttered. "She can't be going far."

Debbie passed Sage Advice and I glanced inside to find Annabelle waving at me. I held up a finger, hoping that it signed I'd be back in a minute. As Debbie continued her jaunt, Daisy kept complaining, so I tuned her out.

Where was Lewis' girlfriend headed?

To my surprise, she entered the church. Built when Heywood was first found, the old brick building was once Catholic denomination, but now stood as a secular place of worship headed by the very amicable Minister Paul. A young man in his twenties with a head of black hair, a strong jawline and a Hollywood smile, the women of Heywood flocked to church to hear the word of God and admire his looks.

What was Debbie doing there? Obviously, if she was messing around with a married man, she fell into the so-called sinner category. Maybe she was confessing her adultery?

"It's really none of my business what she's

doing," I said to Daisy as we stood in the parking lot.

"No, it's not. What is your business is that your dog is freezing and I think you need to buy me a coat."

"Okay, sorry. We can't stand out here without looking very conspicuous, and you aren't allowed in the church."

"They should allow dogs in the church," Daisy said. "Do you know what 'dog' spelled backwards is?"

"Yes. God."

"Exactly. We belong there. Or I should say, *I* belong there. You, I'm not so sure about."

While ignoring her slam on me, I couldn't argue that dogs didn't belong in church. Having a few canines wandering around to be petted could be very soothing.

Daisy continued, "Maybe if they allowed me in, I could use my super sniffer in there and catch Debbie's scent, then you could take me to the hardware store and I could see if I can match it. Then the case would be over, and I'd be the big hero!"

"All hail Daisy's super sniffer," I said, chuckling.

"Yes! Daisy's the best crime fighter, ever!" She sat down and stared up at me with a pleading gaze. "Can we go see Jack now? He's my friend, not like those two jerks at home."

I turned and headed down the sidewalk back toward Sage Advice. "Daisy, you're going to have to get over the fact they don't want anything to do with you. Just ignore them. Hopefully, they'll be adopted soon."

If that was going to happen, I needed to post in my social media groups. I should've done that first thing that morning, but I'd been so consumed thinking about Molly's murder, it hadn't occurred to me. I pulled out my phone and set a reminder on my calendar for later this afternoon to let the social media groups know I had quite the pair ready for adoption.

Annabelle greeted me with a squeal and a big hug. I tried not to bristle at her touch. By now, I should be used to her enthusiastic hello, but I wasn't a hugger.

"Unleash me! Unleash me!" Daisy yelled. "I have to find Jack!"

I bent over and unhooked her, then she bolted from the main store into the back room. Glancing around, I took in the beautiful displays of handmade tinctures, soaps and shampoos Annabelle had arranged while inhaling the fresh scent of citrus.

"It smells like summer in here," I noted.

"It's so cold out, I thought I'd bring in some warmer vibes." She flipped her crimped hair over her shoulder, then crossed her arms over her chest. "It was either, like, citrus or coconut, and Doug said coconut was too much."

"Where is he?" I asked. Doug had once been a homeless drug addict and literally lived under a bridge by the Riverwalk. With Annabelle's help, he'd cleaned himself up.

"Grocery store," Annabelle said. "I'm just about to have some dandelion tea. I'm trying to purge the junk in my liver from the holidays. Do you want some?"

Drinking weed water was not my thing. "I'm good."

I followed her to the back room and took a seat on a stool as she poured her tea. Her workspace was filled with different herbs and spices and I wished I could stomach her fabulous teas. With our town doctor being murdered a while back, Annabelle had become the person to see when one of our residents became ill. She'd done a wonderful job stepping in.

We chatted for a few moments as the dogs ran up and down the stairs playing chase. When the chimes sounded, indicating someone had come in the door, Annabelle stood and hurried to the front of the store.

"Hi there!" Annabelle chirped. "Can I help you?"

"Where is she?" the woman asked. "I saw her come in here!"

"Who? Gina?"

My heart skipped a beat at the sound of my name. I stood and walked to the front to find Debbie with her hands fisted at her sides, her cheeks rosy red, and I guessed that wasn't from the cool weather. My stomach curled with worry.

"Stop it!" she yelled. "Leave me out of this!"

"What are you talking about?" I asked, my anxiety turning to curiosity.

"I saw you following me to the church! Are you spreading your gossip? How I was involved with a married man? Is that what you're doing? Maybe you'll even contact the paper! Take out an ad about my love for Lewis!"

She shook her head and let out a guttural scream. Turing, she stormed out, leaving me speechless. Both of us stared at the door.

After a long moment, Annabelle asked, "What was that all about?"

"I'm... I'm not sure," I replied. "I went with Trevor to talk to her about her sleeping with Lewis Burton, and now she thinks I was following her."

"Well, didn't you?" Annabelle asked. "I saw you, like, walk by right after she did."

I waved my hand in front of my face. "Okay, I was following her, but that's beside the point."

"I don't get it. She said you were following her, and you were. Where did she go?"

"To the church."

"So, what's the big deal?" Annabelle asked. "I'm so, like, confused. Why is she yelling at you like that?"

Was Debbie simply paranoid her secret would get out and she'd be potentially shamed, or was she trying to make me feel bad about my actions so I wouldn't continue to look into her whereabouts the night Molly was murdered?

"I don't know, Annabelle, but I've had this feeling she was hiding something, and now I'm almost sure of it."

CHAPTER 9

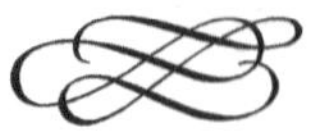

TREVOR PHONED me on my way back to my car.

"Where are you?" he asked.

"I just visited Annabelle," I replied. "And I had a really strange thing happen. I saw Debbie"

"Come down to On The River," Trevor interrupted. "We can have a quick brunch and talk."

"Are you there now?"

"Yes. I just sat down. I don't even have a cup of coffee in front of me."

I glanced at Daisy. What would I do with her? It was too cold to leave her in the car, however if I left the heat on, she should be fine. I didn't have to stay with Trevor very long.

"Okay, I'll be there in a few. Make sure you're at a table where I can see the parking lot. Daisy's going to be in the car and I need to keep an eye on her."

"No problem. The windows overlooking the Riverwalk are pretty drafty at this time of year, so the parking lot it is."

I hung up and hurried over to the car while explaining to Daisy what I was going to do. "I won't be long," I said, firing up the engine.

"That's okay, Gina. Even though dogs should be allowed everywhere, I'm ready for a nap and I don't feel like arguing."

Thank goodness.

I drove over to On The River, pulled into a parking space next to the windows and noticed Trevor waving from inside. I smiled and exited the car. Realizing I was excited to see him, I wondered if it was because of the case, or if my feelings for him may be growing beyond friendship.

After pulling open the door, a blast of warm air engulfed me. A large fire danced in the stone fireplace and the low hum of many conversations filled the cozy restaurant. Glancing over at where Sally's chef had been murdered, I could still envision the body lying over the table, despite the nice couple who were eating there. With a shiver, I unzipped my coat and headed over to where Trevor sat.

"Hi!" I greeted him, smiling.

"Hey, Gina. Thanks for meeting me." He stood and took my coat, then hung it on the hook next to the booth. Who said chivalry was dead?

"Sure. What's up? Did you talk to Bryce Willis?"

"No. He's been a difficult man to track down."

Just then the owner, Sally, came over to the table, set down a coffee pot and two mugs, then turned to me. "Gina! It's so good to see you!"

Sally was also a hugger, and I tried not to flinch as she took me into an embrace. Afterward, I slid into the booth.

"Aren't you two cute," she said, pushing her glasses up her beak-like nose. "You know, this is where Sam and Jordan used to sit when they came. You remind me so much of them."

Heat flamed my cheeks. Both used to live in Heywood. Sam had been from Hollywood, while Jordan was a sheriff's deputy. They'd fallen in love, and when Sam had come into more money than she knew what to do with, they'd taken off to travel the world.

Sam had also helped Jordan with police business, so I understood my relationship with Trevor mirrored theirs, except I wasn't in love with Trevor.

Not in the least bit.

Well, I wouldn't know what being in love felt like, anyway.

"Have you heard from them at all?" Sally asked.

Both Trevor and I shook our heads.

"I got a postcard from Fiji from Sam," Sally said. "They're doing well and will be back in town in the next month or two."

"It'll be nice to see them," Trevor said.

"We can all live vicariously through their travel stories," Sally said, shaking her head. "I would sure like a little beach sand beneath my toes right now."

"You could clear off the snow down at the river," I kidded.

"And get frostbite in her toes," Trevor replied. "That's the last thing she needs."

We chatted a few more minutes about how nice warm sun on our skin would feel, then Sally said, 'What can I get you two? Gina, are you up for the regular?"

"Yes, please." I'd never turn down on of Sally's breakfast burrito.

"I'll have the Giant All-American," Trevor said. "With a little extra gravy on those biscuits, please."

How the man stayed thin, I'd never understand. He ate like a bear just out of hibernation.

"Sounds good," Sally said. "Be back in a jiffy."

After she left, Trevor pulled out his phone. "I just need to look at my notes before I talk to you. I don't want to get anything wrong."

While waiting, I poured us each a cup of coffee and added two sugars to his, just the way he liked it. I stuck with cream.

"Okay, so here's the deal," Trevor said.

"I'm waiting on phone records for Molly and Lewis."

"What about Debbie?"

"Yes, her as well, but I'm more interested in the Burtons. Anyway, I had a chance to go through some financials on Hammer and Nail, and I found something interesting."

Could it be more interesting than my recent run-in with Debbie? "What's that?"

"There's a vendor who supplies the handmade metal signs. Have you seen them?"

Mostly I went in for dog treats or things I needed for DIY repairs. Handmade metal signs weren't on my radar. "I have no idea what you're talking about."

He chuckled, then sighed. "So, he does different signs. Geoff Longhorn is his name. There are some outlines of dogs. He also does address numbers. Some that read 'welcome.' It's my understanding that he also does custom work which can be ordered through the store. In a nutshell, he does decorations for the home."

I shrugged, surprised I hadn't noticed the dogs. "Okay, what about him?"

"The Burtons hadn't paid him for the

things they'd sold in four months. They owed him close to five thousand dollars."

"Wow. The art must be popular."

"It is. I'm surprised you don't have any, especially the dog pieces. I frequently see his work around town."

At times like these, I wondered what business I had trying to solve a murder. I was in Hammer and Nail a couple times a week and I hadn't noticed this art that everyone in town seemed to have, except for me. I was the local dog rescuer. Those amazing dog pieces should've been something I'd observe.

"Why hadn't they paid him?" I asked.

"Your guess is as good as mine, but after we eat, I was thinking we could go talk with Lewis first, and then Geoff."

It would be interesting to hear why Lewis hadn't paid Geoff and what Lewis had to say about the slight... but what about my dog? I couldn't drop her back at the house or her sassy mouth would get her in trouble with Frank and Marilyn. "I have to bring Daisy," I said. "We have a little issue at home, and I can't leave her there."

"What's going on?"

As I carefully treaded through the story, making sure not to mention that Daisy had had conversations with the dogs, I explained Frank and Marilyn's bond. "They're cute, but they don't want anything to do with Daisy, which upsets her."

"And you're aware of this because she told you?" Trevor said, chuckling.

Dang it. "Of course not," I replied, rolling my eyes. "It's just obvious. She tries to be friendly, and the little one, Frank, growls at her."

"It sounds like you need to find a place for them without any other animals."

"Agreed."

"Well, I'm sure Daisy will be happy to tag along," Trevor said just as Sally approached and set down our plates. My mouth watered as I studied my beloved breakfast burritos. Trevor's breakfast consisted of eggs, bacon, sausage, pancakes, and biscuits with gravy. I couldn't imagine trying to consume all of it, but I also knew from experience that there'd be nothing left.

"Here you go!" Sally said. "Can I get you anything else?"

Trevor and I exchanged glances, and I shook my head. "I think we're good. Thanks, Sally. This looks amazing!"

"Of course it is," she said. "I made it."

I laughed as she winked, then she scurried away.

As I dove in, I felt someone staring at me. I glanced up at Trevor, but he was busy inhaling his mountain of food. I turned to the window and found Daisy standing on the center console, glaring at me. If I could've heard her, I imagined she'd be yelling at me to save her some burrito. Guilt washed through me. Why wasn't she sleeping instead of watching me eat?

"What happened with Debbie?" Trevor asked.

Between bites, I explained how I'd followed her to the church, and then gave him the details of the confrontation in Sage Advice. "It was over the top," I said. "Even Annabelle was surprised by her outburst."

"If Annabelle thinks someone's behavior is over the top, it must be," Trevor said. "She's set quite the high bar."

"Exactly."

Daisy's gaze sat firmly on me as I wolfed down my food. Every few minutes I'd glance out the window to check on her. Her stare annoyed me to no end. So much for a peaceful meal.

"Are you ready?" I asked, even though he clearly wasn't. Two biscuits with gravy, four slices of bacon and a half-eaten pancake still sat on his plate.

"No."

Although I tried to remain calm, my knee bounced under the table as I drank my coffee. Was Daisy too hot in the car? Or was she simply trying to annoy me? Maybe I needed to check on her.

"I'll be right back," I muttered, then hurried from the restaurant. Daisy's tail wagged as I approached and opened the door. "What's wrong?"

"Did you save me any breakfast burrito?" she asked. "I've been such a good dog sitting here and watching you, I think I deserve some."

"Okay, can you quit with the staring? You're making me nervous."

"And you're making me hungry. Please bring me some burrito."

I shut the door and returned inside. That dang dog.

"Everything okay?" Trevor asked.

"Fine." I slipped back into the booth. "I was worried she was too warm."

"It looked like you were talking to her."

I shrugged. "I was. You know I always talk to dogs."

With a chuckle, he set down his fork on his clean plate. "Are we ready to go?"

"We're heading to see Lewis and Geoff Longhorn, right?"

"Yes, ma'am." His smiled faded while he stared at me.

"What's wrong?"

"Gina, I know you told me you don't want me to tell you anything about your mom, but I have information that I think you need to hear."

His words slammed into me like a fist to the gut. "She's alive?"

"Yes."

My breath caught in my throat as I curled my hands into fists under the table. Did I want to be privy to the information? I wasn't sure. I could barely wrap my mind around the fact that she was alive and hadn't contacted me in decades after leaving my brother and me one afternoon under the guise of going to the store. I understood that her life had been in danger, but what had she been doing? She could've sent a birthday card, a Christmas card, a smoke signal... anything.

I stood, grabbed my coat and slipped it on. "Not now, Trevor. I can't deal with this."

"Gina, I—"

"Please, don't. I know I asked you to find out anything you could about her, and I appreciate that you did, but I can't think about her right now."

"Can't, or won't?" he asked gently. He stood and placed his hands on my shoulders. "You have to confront that awful time in your history at some point."

"And that's not now," I said, pulling away from him. "I'd rather catch a killer."

Frankly, I'd rather put my foot in a wood-chipper than deal with news about my mother.

CHAPTER 10

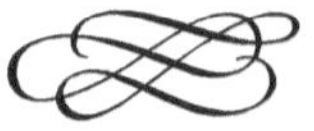

I REMEMBER the day my mother—Brandy Dunner had been her name—had left. Felt like it had been yesterday. Vic had always blamed himself because he'd told her she was fat and he had refused to empty the dishwasher. Then she'd said she was going to the store and we never saw or heard from her again.

I hadn't realized it at the time, but the aftermath had been very traumatic. Growing up as a wild child without rules or boundaries had been difficult as I attempted to navigate becoming a woman. Especially living in a house where I'd been relentlessly teased by my brother and my father had been trying to keep a roof over our heads and food on our table. The fact he'd been doing that by selling drugs still didn't sit right with me, and I assumed it never would.

Maybe after I found who killed Molly I'd discover what Trevor knew about Brandy, who was alive. I wasn't sure how I felt about that. It seemed easier to think of her as dead, and that she didn't have any opportunity over the past decades to reach out and apologize for abandoning her children.

"You okay?" Trevor asked.

I glanced over at the driver's seat and instead of seeing him, I found my dog standing on the console between us, her tongue hanging out as she stared at me.

"Gina seems sad," she said. "Doesn't she, Trevor?" Daisy always spoke to him as if he could hear her.

"I'm fine," I grumbled. "Just thinking about who might've killed Molly."

We drove down Comfort Road, then suddenly Trevor yanked the steering wheel to the left. "Looks like Lewis is at Hammer and Nail."

"You released the crime scene?" I asked.

"Sure did. I called him this morning to let him know."

"He didn't waste any time getting back in there," I muttered.

"Nope. He's got a lot of clean-up to do and then he's got to open for business, especially if he owes one vendor five-thousand dollars."

We pulled into the parking spot next to what I assumed to be Lewis' truck. I jumped out of Trevor's too high vehicle and Daisy followed.

"You need to stay here," I said, pointing at the seats she'd just left.

"No. I'm going in with you. I promise to be a good dog."

"They don't allow dogs in the hardware store," I said. "Get back in the car."

"What did I say before?" Daisy asked. "What's dog spelled backward?"

"I'm aware, but even a holy deity like you can't come in. No dogs."

After a long glare, she jumped back into the truck and I slammed the door. I turned to find Trevor staring at me.

"You just had a full-on conversation with

her," he said, his brow furrowing. "Do I need to be concerned?"

Caught again. Maybe one day I'd have to level with him and tell the truth. For now, I'd turn the tables. "You must be hearing things. I simply told her she can't go inside and to get back into the truck."

"And you think she understood that?"

"Well, she's back inside, right?" I shrugged. "She understands some things. It's not like I'm discussing physics or the meaning of God with her."

Even though we'd sort of had that conversation, but I'd ignore that part.

"Yeah, but Gina, you were—"

"Let's go inside, okay? It's freezing out here."

I made a big deal of blowing into my hands and jumping up and down as if to show that if I stopped moving, I'd become an ice sculpture.

"Come on," he grumbled.

I followed him inside. The usually busy store was silent and had a chill in the air. With the lights off and dim sunbeams coming through the windows, it felt as if I'd just walked into a scene from a horror movie. I fully expected someone to burst from an aisle with a chainsaw. Thankfully, Trevor was leading the way and I could run really fast if needed. As we passed the broom display, I considered picking one up for self-defense, but then I realized my imagination was probably getting the best of me. And besides, a broom against a chainsaw wielding psycho? I didn't stand a chance.

"Lewis?" Trevor called. "You around?"

Noise filtered from the back office, and Trevor headed that way. As we passed the obvious crime scene, I tried not to look. However, the dried blood, broken glass and miscellaneous tools scattered across the floor held my attention.

"Lewis?" Trevor yelled again. "It's Deputy Trevor Hutchison. Can we come back?"

Footsteps sounded down the hall and seconds later, Lewis rounded the corner. "Hey, Deputy," he said, running a hand over the sides of his head where what little hair he had left resided. "I wasn't expecting you today."

"I was up the street and saw your car,"

Trevor said, his hand settling on top of his gun, as if he felt threatened. "Everything okay here?"

"Fine, fine. What can I do for you?"

The middle-aged man with the pot belly did seem nervous and disheveled. Sweat dotted his brow and his shirt was half-out of his jeans.

A loud *bang* came from the back room. The three of us turned toward the sound.

"What was that?" Trevor asked. "Is someone here with you?"

"No! No, no one is here. I had leaned a ladder against the wall. It must've fallen. Now, what can I do for you?"

"I wanted to thank you for allowing me to take a peek at your financials," Trevor said. His gaze darted to the open door leading to the back hallway while his hand continued to sit on top of his holster. "I did have one question after going through them, though."

"Sure. What's up?" Lewis wiped his hand across his forehead then crossed his arms over his chest.

"Tell me about Geoff Longhorn."

As Lewis' brow furrowed, another noise

came from down the hall. Or was I hearing things?

"What about him? He supplies the metal artwork here at the store. To my surprise, we sell quite a bit of it."

"You sell it, but you don't pay him?" I asked. Trevor shot me a glare, clearly conveying I should keep my mouth shut, and he was right. I was only along for the ride, but oftentimes I spoke before I thought.

"What do you mean I don't pay him?" Lewis asked.

"The store owes him over five thousand dollars," I replied, ignoring Trevor's silent warning.

"What?!" Lewis shrieked. "What are you talking about?"

"Can we go into your office and talk about it?" Trevor asked.

Lewis shook his head. "There's nowhere to sit. I'm cleaning out the space, trying to figure out what Molly had been up to."

For some reason, I didn't believe him. Perhaps it was all the noise from the back room, or maybe the sweat that streamed from his brow, but Lewis was lying.

"Is there a reason why Geoff wasn't paid?" Trevor asked.

"Molly came in a few months ago and basically took over all the invoicing and inventory," Lewis said. "The only thing I could think of is that she decided not to pay him for some reason."

"Are there other outstanding invoices?" I asked.

Lewis shrugged. "Like I said, I'm trying to figure all that out, but the phone call I received the other day makes a lot more sense."

"What phone call?" Trevor asked. "Who was it?"

"It was Geoff," Lewis said. "He told me that if he didn't get paid, I'd be sorry."

A chill ran down my spine as I glanced over my shoulder to where Molly had died. Was Geoff responsible for the murder? Had he done it because he was owed money?

"And what did you tell him?" Trevor asked.

"I said I had no idea what he was talking about, but I'd be happy to put him in touch with Molly. I looked around the store for her, but she'd left while I was trying to work the cash register and help customers find some things... I was swamped. I told Geoff Molly would call him back."

"And did she?" I asked.

"I forgot he called," Lewis muttered. "I never told Molly about it. And it never crossed my mind again until you just mentioned him."

When he wiped his sweaty brow again, I narrowed my gaze. I felt he was lying about something, but what was it? Was there someone hiding in back? Or was he bluffing about Geoff calling, maybe setting up the man to take the fall for Molly's death? We needed to speak to Geoff to verify that he'd made his veiled threat against Lewis. Even if he didn't admit it, Trevor could look into the phone records of both parties.

"You better cut him a check," I said. "Based on what you've told us, he's pretty upset."

"I would be in his shoes as well," Lewis replied, then turned his attention to Trevor. "Is there anything else I can do for you, deputy?"

Trevor stared at the man for a long moment, then shook his head. He still kept his hand on his holster, so I guessed he was most likely thinking the same thing I was—something wasn't right in this situation. But what was it?

"There's one other thing," Trevor said. "I was wondering why you didn't tell me about your affair with Debbie Williams?"

As the color drained from his face, he glanced to the back office.

"I see," I said, now fully understanding what he was lying about. "She's here, isn't she?"

His wide stare was the only answer I needed.

I shook my head. "You know, you could at least wait until Molly's body was cold before bringing in Debbie to help you with the business."

"It's... it's not what it looks like," he stammered.

"Well... I think it's exactly what it looks like," I said. "You were having an affair with Debbie and you wanted Molly out of the picture." I shrugged. "Seems pretty cut and dried to me."

Lewis glanced over his shoulder again, then sighed. "My marriage was on the rocks. Molly was having an affair... our marriage was basically over."

"Why didn't you divorce?" Trevor asked.

"I honestly don't know."

"Maybe because it would be a financial mess?" I asked. "Maybe you didn't want to lose the store?"

Lewis stared at his shoes for a long moment, then nodded. "That probably had something to do with it."

"And now Molly is out of the way," I said.

"Look," Lewis said, pointing his finger at me. "My marriage to Molly was over, but that doesn't mean I wanted her dead."

"Her death sure solved a lot of your problems," Trevor pointed out.

"It did, but I swear to you, I didn't kill her. I'm not a violent man."

For some reason, I didn't quite believe him.

CHAPTER 11

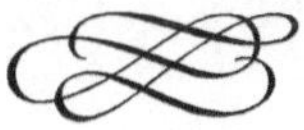

As Trevor and I walked out of Hammer and Nail, he turned to me. "That was an interesting interaction."

"I agree." My insides buzzed with excitement. "Debbie is trying to hide their affair, but she was there, Trevor."

"I know. I figured it was either her or a nest of rabid squirrels in the back room."

"Then why did you have your hand on your gun? It seemed like you felt threatened."

He chuckled and shook his head. "I wasn't worried. I kept it there because it makes me look cool. And besides, have you ever seen a rabid squirrel? Those things scare me."

I burst out laughing as we got in the car.

"Someone had a fun trip into the hardware store," Daisy said. "Without taking me, God's favorite creature."

"Oh, stop it," I hissed just as Trevor opened the door.

"Trevor! Trevor!" Daisy yelled. "I was such a good girl! I wanted to chew on this seatbelt back here but I didn't!"

"Are we still heading to Geoff's house?" I asked, shooting her a glare.

"Heck, yes," Trevor said, firing up the truck. "I love it when it feels like an investigation is coming together."

I arched an eyebrow, unsure how he felt the investigation was moving forward. As far as I was concerned, I was more confused than ever, but based on the conversation we'd just had, Lewis had moved to the top of my list. He had plenty of motive, as well as opportunity. "How is this coming together?"

"Well, in the beginning, I didn't really have any suspects. I had some ideas, sure, but the further we get into the weeds, suspects are popping up like wildflowers, along with great motives. It'll break wide open soon."

He sounded so certain, but I supposed he had to keep the faith. I couldn't imagine being fully responsible for finding a killer and failing. That would eat me alive. I was only his trusty sidekick, not the one who would get the accolades for solving the case. "I really like Lewis for it," I said. "But he also owes Geoff a lot of money, which makes me wonder about him."

"I bet it's this guy we're going to see," Daisy said. "Money is a great reason to kill someone!"

Furrowing my brow, I glanced out the passenger window again. My dog said things that often mirrored my own thoughts. Was I having conversations with myself? Did I possess a split personality disorder? I didn't want to think about that, either.

We pulled up in front of Geoff Longhorn's green house with white trim. The front yard was littered with metal artwork—everything from a life-sized giraffe to a quail family peeking out from under the snow. I wondered what else sat beneath the white stuff.

The driveway hadn't been shoveled, and there wasn't any sign of a walkway.

"I guess we'll just do our best not to step on anything," I said. "Hopefully we can find a path."

Trevor jumped out the truck and I followed, muttering to Daisy to keep her butt exactly where it was.

"Maybe I will chew up this seatbelt, Gina! Then you'll be sorry!"

I slammed the door and stood next to Trevor at the curb. I wasn't pleased with Daisy's behavior in the least bit. The only thing I could attribute it to were the dogs at home. Perhaps she was taking her frustration with them out on me?

"I'm guessing we'll find a path right around here," he said.

"Hopefully, you're right," I replied. "I'd hate to step on something beneath the snow and ruin it."

"Or trip and fall and break a leg," he sighed.

"Yes. That, too."

"Here goes nothing."

It was good I was trailing him because

he'd be responsible for destroying the hidden artwork beneath the snow if he took a misstep, and he'd be the one with the broken leg, not me. I didn't have time for injuries.

I followed him up the walkway to the door without tripping or stepping on anything, to my surprise. "Nicely done," I said as he rang the doorbell.

"Thank you. I'm glad I could impress you today. Hopefully it won't be the last time."

I smiled and glanced up at him and he gave me a quick wink. A slow blush crawled over my neck as my stomach twisted uncomfortably. Was he flirting with me? Please, no. But oddly enough, a small part of me wanted him to be doing just that. Goodness, I didn't need to be thinking about romantic entanglements, either.

Thankfully, the front door opened and I was able to push my uneasiness to the side and concentrate on the reason we'd come.

The tall, thin man had long black hair with gray strands draping over his shoulders and was of Native American descent. I guessed his age somewhere in his sixties. "What can I do for you?" he asked.

"Geoff Longhorn, I assume?" Trevor flashed his badge.

"Yes."

"Geoff, who is it?" A woman's voice called from inside.

"The police!" he yelled back.

"Oh, my word!" A moment later, a Native American woman appeared next to him. Short and thin, also with long black hair, her brow furrowed as she took us in. "What's this about?"

"We don't know," Geoff growled. "If you shut your mouth, Wanda, maybe we'll find out."

I pursed my lips and fought the urge to slap him across the face. With the experience my now dead ex-husband had given me, I could spot an abusive relationship with ease.

"Oh, shut up, you old grump," she said. "What can we do for you, officers?"

Ha! They thought I was police. *Excellent.* "Do you two always talk to each other like that?" I blurted out.

"We've been married for thirty-two years," the woman said, rolling her eyes. "After that much time, you can't stand each other, but it's too much trouble to part ways. Now, what do you two want?"

I pondered her explanation while Trevor glared at me. I wouldn't want to be in a marriage like that whether it was thirty-two years or thirty-two seconds. Having already had more than my fair share of toxic relationships, that's probably why I preferred the company of dogs instead.

"We understand that Lewis Burton over at Hammer and Nail Hardware owed you money," Trevor said. "I was hoping to ask you a couple questions about that."

"Sure," Geoff said, leaning against the doorframe. "What about it?"

For some reason, I thought they'd invite Trevor and me inside instead of all of us standing on the porch in the frigid cold. The urge to jump up and down to warm myself was strong as a deep chill rolled down my spine, making it seem as if my bones were shaking.

"Was this the first time Lewis had shorted you?" Trevor asked.

"No. He's done it before. This time was different, though."

"Why is that?" Trevor asked.

"Because in the past, it had always just been a mistake. Not this time."

"I don't know about that, Geoff," Wanda said. "At least, it didn't seem like it was Lewis' fault."

"Well, you might be right on that," Geoff muttered. "But it still doesn't make it right."

"Can you tell us what happened?" Trevor urged.

"I didn't get paid," Geoff said. "I called the store a few times and spoke to Molly. She said she'd get right on it, apologized a lot, then never sent me a check."

"Did you feel it was intentional?" I asked.

Geoff sighed and crossed his arms over his chest. "At first, no. Then, after the third or fourth call, I began to think it was."

"But it was Molly, not Lewis," Wanda interjected. "She was the one this last time who wasn't paying us."

"I don't know about that," Geoff said. "That's your stance, Wanda. I think both of them are more crooked than a couple of sidewinder snakes."

"Sorry, I'm confused," I said. "Did you

think Lewis was in on holding your money, or not?"

"I don't know. But I do know for sure I called Molly many times and she kept promising me she'd get around to it and she never did. I would think she'd tell her husband that I wanted to be paid, which makes him guilty as well. He should've written a check out to me the first time she said something."

"What if I told you that Lewis had no idea he was behind on payment until today?" Trevor asked.

Doubt flickered in Geoff's gaze as Wanda's mouth fell open.

"I understand that you made a phone call to Lewis a couple of days ago," Trevor continued. "And I believe you said something to the effect that if you didn't get paid, Lewis would be sorry."

"Maybe I did say something like that," Geoff grunted. "So what? I've got bills to pay, just like everyone else."

"Did you happen to mean that if he didn't pay, you'd kill Molly?" I asked.

The color drained from Geoff's face.

"You know Molly's dead, right?" Trevor asked.

Wanda slapped Geoff on the shoulder. "What the heck is wrong with you, you idiot? You *threatened* Lewis? And now Molly's dead?"

"I never hurt Molly," Geoff said quickly. "Never. I can't believe you're here accusing me of such a thing!"

"We aren't accusing you of anything," Trevor said gently. "We're asking questions in the hopes of finding Molly's killer."

"You've darkened the wrong door!" Wanda shouted. "Get out of here!"

Trevor sighed. "Ma'am, I wanted—"

"I don't give a darn what you wanted," Wanda hissed, waving her finger in front of Trevor's face. "You don't come to *my* house and accuse *my* husband of murder."

"As I said, I just wanted to ask a few questions," Trevor said. "No one is accusing anyone of anything."

Wanda's bluster seemed to slowly deflate, but then she shook her head. "You aren't asking anyone anything until we talk to a lawyer."

She shoved Geoff inside then slammed the door in our faces.

As I stared at the panel, Trevor swore under his breath.

"That didn't go well," I said.

"Very observant," he sighed. "Come on, let's go."

We shuffled back down the path. As I slid into the truck, Daisy asked, "Why was that lady yelling at you? She was so mad. Almost as mad as me."

"You better not have chewed up a seatbelt," I muttered. "Or I'll be madder than you and that woman combined."

Trevor opened the door, entered the cab and started the truck. Heat blasted from the vents and I placed my hands over them.

"What do you think that was about?" he asked.

I shrugged and pursed my lips. "Well, maybe Geoff did kill Molly because he didn't get paid, and Wanda knows it."

"She was so defensive," Trevor replied.

I nodded and stared out the windshield while appreciating whoever invented the heating mechanism in vehicles. I still found it odd that they let us stand out on the porch instead of inviting us in. "Wanda seems like she may wear the pants in the family," I said. "Now, I'm just thinking out loud, but what if they were working together? Wanda was aware of the threat and then they killed Molly? Was anything else missing from the store? Was there a robbery?"

Trevor pulled out his notebook. "Yes. According to Lewis, there was approximately three thousand dollars in cash missing."

"Well, there you go. They killed Molly to send a message and took the money to pay their bills."

"I don't know," Trevor said. "What if—"

With a gasp, I turned to him. "What if Wanda took matters into her own hands?"

"You mean, she killed Molly?"

"Yes. And now she's upset that the police are asking questions."

"She's so small and thin, though," he said. "Do you think she's got the strength to kill like that?"

"Molly died by being beaten to death with a hammer." I sat back against the seat and Daisy licked the side of my face. As I pushed her away, I recalled Erika's video of slamming the pink hammer against the nail. "It doesn't take strength to do that. One surprise hit, and Molly could've been down. Finishing her off would have been easy."

"You're right," Trevor murmured. "So now I have to add Wanda to my list of suspects."

"If you're a decent cop, then yes. I don't understand why she'd react like that unless either she or Geoff killed Molly... or they planned the murder together."

CHAPTER 12

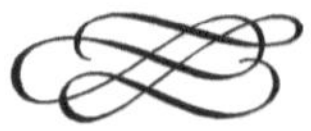

WHEN DAISY and I arrived home, my thoughts were elsewhere and I'd momentarily forgotten about my guests, Frank and Marilyn. That was until I heard growling from the living room.

I hurried in there to find Frank and Marilyn exactly where we'd left them. The only difference was Frank was standing and had placed himself in between Daisy and Marilyn. Daisy darted around the room trying to bypass him and get to the shepherd.

"Just let me by, Napoleon," she said, running to the left. "I want to be her friend!"

The growling had escalated to teeth baring. As I tried to hide a smile—it was hard to take the ferocity of the little dachshund seriously—I said, "Okay, everyone outside for a pee, please."

Daisy hurried to the back door. "This is my chance, Gina! Marilyn is going to become my friend outside and we're going to run and play and the little tyrant will eat my dust!"

I opened the door and the three dogs filed out. Daisy went first, then Frank, followed by Marilyn. Daisy did a quick zoomie around the yard, then faced off with the other two who were sniffing the fence line.

"Let's play, Marilyn!" She leaned on her front legs and placed her butt up in the air, her tail wagging so fast, it was a brown and white blur. "Come on, chase me! We'll leave that little brat behind!"

As Daisy attempted to entice Marilyn into a game of chase, I pursed my lips while watching them through the window. Marilyn glanced over at Daisy every couple of moments, and once or twice, she actually tried to trot toward my dog, but was stopped by Frank.

Daisy bounded around them as Frank

nipped at her, always placing himself between the two females.

"What a little jerk," I muttered. After a few moments, Daisy lowered her head and slowly walked to the back door. I opened it and let her in.

"They don't like me," she pouted, her head down.

I held the door open for a few seconds to see if Frank and Marilyn wanted to come in. They continued their exploration of the fence line while I tried to placate my dog with lies. "I don't think it's that they don't like you. I think it's more about them trying to become comfortable in our house."

"Gina, you can't understand dog talk, only human talk. They told me just now that they don't like me."

"They said that in dog language?"

"Yes. They're mean. Especially little Frank."

I didn't know what to say to make her feel better. "I'm sorry, Daisy."

"I'm going to the bedroom. Let me know when you find them a new home. And try really hard to do that, Gina."

With her tail between her legs and her head hanging, she walked down the hallway, defeated. The last rescue that had come through our house had been an unruly golden retriever. She'd also wanted him gone, but mainly because he was destructive and a general pain. He hadn't been mean, not as she claimed Frank and Marilyn had been.

I snapped a few pictures of the bonded pair outside, then sat down at the kitchen table and pulled out my phone. After firing up my social media apps, I posted about the two, making it clear they'd need to stay together and go to a home free of other dogs and kids. After a few minutes, I noted my posts had been shared a couple of times. I set down my phone and prayed the power of social media would help me out.

Now, back to the murder.

Trevor hadn't been very clear on why he hadn't talked to Molly's boyfriend, Bryce Willis. I should've pressed him for a reason, but regardless, that needed to be done. Perhaps Molly had decided she was finished with him, and he'd gotten revenge. Lewis had mentioned that she'd told him she was breaking it off...

With so many thoughts swirling, I decided I needed to write some of them out. As someone who loved lists, I pulled out one of my many notebooks and jotted down everything I felt needed to be done to find the killer, as well as miscellaneous thoughts as they came.

1. *Interview Bryce*
2. *We knew Debbie was with Lewis at the store earlier, so we also knew she was lying about not hearing from him since Molly's death. Or, maybe when we talked to her at Diamond Ranch she hadn't heard from him yet??*
3. *Get Geoff's phone records to check his call history. Maybe police can trace his whereabouts the night of Molly's death?*
4. *Was there a man Erika saw in the hallway when she returned to ask Molly for her job back? If there was one, who was it?*

5. *Did Debbie really have a cat, or were the scratches from her fighting with Molly while trying to kill her?*

6. *Why did Erika delete the TikTok video of her using the pink hammer?*

7. *Did Wanda have a criminal history? Could she have killed Molly because she hadn't paid Geoff?*

8. *Did Geoff have a criminal record?*

9. *Where was Wanda the night Molly was murdered?*

As I STARED at the paper, I realized I had more questions about Geoff and Wanda than I did about any other suspect. Did that mean they were guilty? A little niggling in my gut told me that I really needed to focus on them. Well, the police needed to focus on them, so I should share that thought with Trevor.

I also recognized I didn't have the tools to complete most of my tasks or answer the questions. The majority of it would have to be left up to the police. But there was one thing I could check on, and that was Debbie's supposed cat.

If she was a decent person, she'd have adopted. Well, she could be a decent person and gone through a breeder. I was projecting my own dislike of breeders onto her. There were already too many dogs and cats in the world who needed good homes, so breeders who bred dogs just because they could were not my favorite people. Now, those who bred service and work dogs had my utmost respect because those types of dogs were desperately needed.

But back to my cat hunt.

With a sigh, I pulled up my contacts in my phone and began dialing the rescue organizations and people I knew who took in cats. The first few answered no, but it was nice to catch up with some people I hadn't talked to in months. A couple of my calls went right to voicemail where I left messages, so I moved onto our area's animal control. After I explained what I was looking for, the woman who answered the phone said, "I can't give out private information."

"I'm not looking for private information," I replied. "I'm looking to see if a woman named Debbie Williams adopted a kitten."

"And I can't tell you that unless you're the police," she snapped. "It's our policy."

I sighed and rolled my eyes. "Your policy around cat adoption is ridiculous, and yes, I'm the police. Deputy Dunner. Now, instead of irritating me further, can you look at your records and see if Debbie Williams has adopted a kitten in the past few weeks?"

The hesitation in her voice led me to believe her resolve at following the policies was wavering.

"Where are you located?" she asked.

"Heywood. I haven't got all day. Please grab me that information!"

"One moment. It's going to take some time for me to go through the records."

"I can wait."

As the minutes passed, I glanced outside to find Frank and Marilyn standing at the door, ready to come in. I opened it and they trotted back into the living room and took their places on the couch. Both ignored me.

"Glad to have you two here," I muttered.

"Officer Dunner?" The woman on the phone had returned.

"Yes?"

"Debbie Williams hasn't been in to adopt."

"Okay, thank you."

"I'll need to get your badge number—"

After hanging up, I shook my head. She should've attempted to collect that before she gave me the information I needed.

I glanced at my list again while tapping my pen against the table.

"Can you stop doing that, Gina?" Daisy yelled from down the hall. "You're really starting to irritate me."

With a curse, I stood and opened my refrigerator. I still hadn't been to the store so I had nothing to eat. "Maybe I should do that now," I muttered as my stomach grumbled.

I hurried down the hall to the bedroom. "I need to go to the store," I said to Daisy, who was curled up on the bed. "Come with me."

"Yay! A car ride! I love car rides!" She quickly jumped from the bed and trotted to the front door. Pleased she hadn't argued, I followed and grabbed my purse and coat before she could change her mind.

Once we were in the car and on our way to Timber Trades, the local grocery store, my phone rang. I hated to talk on my phone while I drove—especially when there could be ice on the roads from the cold weather—so I ignored it. My caller could wait a couple more minutes.

The phone rang again as I pulled into the parking lot. I picked it up and glanced at the screen. Sierra the cat rescuer.

"Hey, Sierra!" I greeted her. "How are things going? Did you have a nice holiday?"

I wasn't one for small talk. In fact, I detested it, but I understood that sometimes it was important because a lot of the population seemed to enjoy it. And for some, it was a ritual before getting to the heart of the conversation. It had taken me a long time to realize that when I hadn't participated in small talk, I'd come across as rude.

As I listened to her story of three cats

taking down her Christmas tree, I scrawled out a list of what I needed in the store. It wasn't very substantial. Turkey, cottage cheese and sourdough bread. Maybe I should throw in some salads or fruit?

"Don't forget wine," Daisy said from the backseat. "You and Trevor finished off the bottle Adrienne gave you."

Excellent point.

"So, what can I do for you, Gina?" Sierra asked.

"Oh, well... I was wondering if you have any kittens and if any had been adopted recently by a woman named Debbie Williams."

"I do have a litter and a few were just adopted in the past couple of weeks. Why do you ask?"

Because she's part of a murder investigation and I need to know if the scratches on her hands are from a cat, like she said, or from a fight where she killed a woman?

But I couldn't say that out loud.

"She's... she's a friend of mine. She was talking about adopting a kitten and I gave her your phone number. I was wondering if she'd picked one up."

"Why don't you just ask her?"

"Because... because if she didn't, I wanted to surprise her and get one for her!"

Oh, my goodness. My lies bordered on brilliance.

"You are such a sweet friend," Sierra sighed. "Let me check my records."

"Gina, you should feel guilty for lying," Daisy said. "I never lie."

I rolled my eyes, but remained quiet in case I was on speakerphone or something. Besides, I was trying to clear someone of a murder—or gather evidence against them— depending on how one was to look at the situation. Couldn't my falsehood be excused for that simple reason?

"Good dogs don't lie," she continued. "So if you were a dog, you'd be a very bad dog. Humans don't like bad dogs."

The ethics lessons from my dog began to annoy me so I shot her a glare.

"Here it is!" Sierra said. "Yes, Debbie Williams adopted a cute little tabby about a week and a half ago."

I nodded and pursed my lips, defeat

rolling through me. "Okay, thank you. I appreciate your time."

After we hung up, I stared at the storefront for a long while. Just because Debbie had been telling the truth about a cat adoption didn't mean she hadn't killed Molly. She and Lewis could've been in on it together.

My phone rang again. Trevor.

"Hey," I greeted him. "What's going on?"

"Gina!" he yelled. "You can't go around impersonating a police officer!"

CHAPTER 13

"Oh, he sounds mad," Daisy said. "You *are* a bad dog."

Maybe it would be best if I just hung up and allowed him time to cool down?

"Gina!" Trevor yelled. "Gina, don't you dare hang up on me!"

Ah, he knew me so well. I really wanted to end this call. Instead, I closed my eyes and rubbed my finger between my eyebrows. "I'm sorry," I blurted. "I was trying to help you with the investigation! I never imagined she'd actually check to see if I was lying!"

He muttered a string of curses under his breath. "Impersonating a police officer is a felony, Gina."

Instead of yelling, he'd downgraded to seething. Or was it an upgrade? I wasn't sure what was worse.

"I'm sorry." I opened my eyes and wondered if I'd ever get out of the car. "I had a list of everything that needed to be done, and I realized I couldn't actually do any of it, except call around and see if Debbie had adopted a cat. I had no idea the state shelter would care about credentials and that they'd verify them."

While he breathed heavily, I imagined him pacing back and forth in his office.

"It's not like I was trying to get someone's phone records or social security number," I continued. "I was seeing if Debbie had adopted a cat!" I could still hear him breathing heavily. "I'm sorry, Trevor. Like I said, I was only trying to help you with the investigation."

"What did you find out? Were the scratches from a kitten, or a fight while she was trying to murder Molly?"

"She did adopt a kitten," I replied. "But that doesn't negate the fact she wanted Lewis for herself, and Lewis wanted her. He admitted his marriage was over. They could've killed Molly together."

Trevor sighed. "Promise me you'll never pull that stunt again."

"I promise."

"Gina, you have been a very bad dog today," Daisy chastised. "Just like Frank is."

I shot her a glare. She apparently had more issues with the four-legged guests than I realized.

Returning my attention to Trevor, I said, "I'm at the grocery store. Why don't you come over tonight for dinner?"

"If it's later, that may work. I have to go see Bryce, Molly's boyfriend."

"You finally tracked him down?"

"Yep. His neighbor told me he'd been out hunting and he was expected back today."

"Hunting in this cold weather? I'd think he'd freeze to death."

"Well, there's that point, but also the fact that he left the day Molly's body was discovered, according to the neighbor."

"They said that?" I asked incredulously. "That he left the day his girlfriend was killed?!"

"No. I asked about what day he'd gone out, and the neighbor told me. She didn't say anything about Molly's death, but the math matches up."

"So, what do you think happened? He killed Molly... because she broke up with him? Then he left town?"

"Something like that. It's thin, but I need to ask the questions. According to the text messages they exchanged, he had been begging her to leave Lewis for months."

"And she didn't," I muttered. "Or maybe she did, and Lewis killed her for it."

Trevor sighed again. "Yeah, I'm not feeling too good about this investigation any longer. I'm spinning in circles."

And I had the distinct feeling that he was going to cut me out of the investigation after the felony I'd committed. Instead of calling myself a deputy, I should've bribed the woman at the shelter with cookies or alcohol. Lesson learned.

I didn't want to be pushed to the side. Access to the investigation was important for me, not only because I needed the details for my book, but because I truly wanted to figure out who killed Molly.

"Something will break. Come by for dinner and we'll hash it out," I offered once again. A long beat of silence ensued. Hopefully, my invitations to eat with me would placate him a bit. I'd always heard the way to a man's heart was through his stomach...

Had he hung up on me? *I* would've hung up on me. "Trevor? Are you there?"

"Yes. Go get what you need at the grocery store, then meet me at your house. I want you to go with me to talk to Bryce."

I smiled. "Sure. That sounds good. I'll see you in a bit. Are steaks okay for dinner?"

"I'll never turn down a steak, Gina."

Frankly, neither would I.

"You seem to be able to catch things that I don't," Trevor said as we pulled away from my house. "Like the scratches on Debbie's arms. But that doesn't mean I'm not angry at you for that stunt you pulled. If Mallory was in town and she received that call, she'd have no regrets about locking you up, Gina."

"I know, and I'm sorry," I said for what felt like the millionth time. "I shouldn't have done that, and I swear on my dog's life, I'll never do it again."

Daisy gasped. "Don't you make a promise like that!"

She'd insisted on coming with Trevor and me, and I hadn't argued. Once we'd arrived home from the store, she'd tried to entice Marilyn into playing again and received a snarl from Frank, or as we both had started calling him, Napoleon. Little terrorist.

I hadn't had a chance to check my social media to see if there were any adoption inquiries, but I'd also placed my phone number in the posts, and it had remained quiet. I didn't give up hope, though. Someone, somewhere, was looking for these two dogs. Maybe they didn't even realize it yet, but there would be a match at some point.

We turned onto the bumpy road leading into the trailer park that stood a few miles outside town. As Trevor slowed, he muttered the address we searched for under his breath.

"There it is," I said, pointing out the passenger window. "It's the baby blue one in need of a touch up."

We pulled in front and I was pleased to see the walkway had been shoveled.

"Ready?" Trevor asked.

"Yes."

"You are not a cop, nor do you play one on television, so don't say you are, okay?"

I nodded as Daisy giggled. "I love Trevor," she said. "He's so funny." She came to the front seat and licked his cheek.

"You're so sweet, Daisy," Trevor said as he rubbed behind her ear.

"Let's go," I said. "Daisy, stay here." She didn't argue, which surprised me since she'd been almost combative with the arrival of Frank and Marilyn. I glanced in the back seat and she stared at me, her tongue hanging out. Pure love shone from her gaze, and I knew she'd be nicer once the rescues had found a new home. It wasn't really me she was angry with, but them. I, unfortunately, seemed to be the one taking the brunt of it.

After giving her nose a quick kiss, I exited

the car. I shut the door and stared at the trailer. A bad feeling twisted my gut.

I followed Trevor up the path and stood a bit behind him as he knocked. A man who looked remarkably like Lewis Burton answered, except he was much thinner.

"Who are you?" he asked.

"Bryce Willis?" Trevor said.

"Yeah." He ran his hand over his balding head. "You're here about Molly, right?"

Trevor nodded. "We just wanted to ask you a few questions."

"Sure, sure." He waved us inside. As the warmth engulfed me, I sighed with relief. When would this cold spell end? Spring was around the corner somewhere, and I wished she'd show her face and heat us up.

"I understand you just got back from a hunting trip?" Trevor said as we filed into the tidy living room and sank into the old brown leather couch.

"I did. I go a few times a year, when it's legal, of course."

"Of course." Trevor smiled and clasped his hands together. "Any luck?"

"Got myself a buck. The meat is going to last me months."

As the two chattered on about where Bryce had found his prey, I studied the sparse living room. It felt like a man had lived there for a long time, without the company of a woman. There weren't any pictures of loved ones, no knickknacks... it was a place to exist, not one reflecting love or family.

"What can you tell us about Molly Burton?" Trevor asked, bringing my attention back to the conversation.

"I loved that woman," Bryce said, then he cleared his throat as if he were dislodging tears. "I... I'm devastated that she's gone."

"How long were you two together?" I asked.

"On and off for a couple of years. I wanted her to leave Lewis so we could be an open item, but she said she wouldn't until the time was right."

"What would make the timing right?" I asked.

"She wanted to bring financial security into our relationship." He waved his hand around. "I live on disability, so I don't have much. I was in Iraq, and it messed with my head."

"You saw some combat then?" Trevor asked.

"Yeah, I did. War is ugly." He jerked his head around as if to clear the thoughts that had invaded his brain. "I can't hold down a job very well, so I do some side work here and there. She wanted to be sure we were comfortable."

It made sense. Molly had recently begun to take an interest in the business, so that led me to believe she was getting ready to leave Lewis. When she did, she'd know exactly how much she should get from the business and their personal finances.

"Were you two in the on or off portion of your relationship the day you went hunting?" Trevor asked.

"We'd just gotten back together after the most recent breakup," Bryce replied. "She told me she'd leave him soon."

"Why did you leave town the morning she was found dead?" Trevor asked.

"Because that's the day I was going hunting." Bryce shrugged. "I didn't know she was dead and I didn't find out until I came home today. My neighbor popped by earlier and told me you'd been asking around for me."

As I stared at the man, I wondered if he was being truthful. What a perfect façade he'd created—the poor guy who simply went hunting only to return to discover the love of his life had been killed.

But what if Molly and Bryce were in the "off" part of their relationship, and this time, she'd said it was final? What if he felt that if he couldn't have her, no one could?

"Well, I'm sorry for your loss, Bryce," Trevor said, shaking his head. "We just need to cover all the bases here to discover who killed Molly."

"Of course. I appreciate the effort. Do you want to know what I think?"

"Sure," I said. "Let's hear it."

"It had to be her husband," he replied. "That man was as mean as a cornered badger. She used to tell me all the things they'd fight about. He was always mad at the tone of her voice, said she sounded like a witch. They fought over everything, and the way he treated her... I had the urge to punch that guy right in the face."

"Thanks for sharing that," Trevor said, before standing. I followed suit. "We'll be in touch if we have any other questions for you."

"Let me know what I can do to help," Bryce said. "I loved that woman, and I want her killer brought to justice."

CHAPTER 14

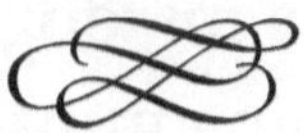

"I don't believe him," I grumbled as Trevor pulled away from the house.

"I wish I could've gotten out of the car so I could've heard what he said," Daisy sighed. "I could've used my super sniffer and maybe we could've solved this case."

"What don't you believe?" Trevor asked.

"It's the perfect set up!" I replied, throwing my hands up in the air. "Can't you see it?"

"No, I can't. Enlighten me."

"Sometimes, Trevor seems kind of dumb," Daisy said.

I couldn't agree more.

"But I still like him," she added. "I like

you, too, Gina, even though I'm mad. I don't like Frank. He's mean."

"He kills Molly because she says they're done," I explained while reaching into the back seat to placate my dog. "Then he disappears—says he's going hunting. When he gets back, he's just a sorry sack who's lost the love of his life and throws Molly's husband under the bus, telling us what a jerk he was to her."

"Well, there *is* a possibility that Lewis is guilty," Trevor argued. "Most of the time it's the husband."

"Does Lewis look like he has a mean bone in his body?" I asked. "Because to me, he seems pretty harmless."

"People aren't themselves while in the heat of hammering someone to death, Gina."

"Yeah, Gina," Daisy said. "Now *you* sound kind of dumb."

I shot my dog a glare and in return, she licked my face while giggling. Sometimes, I think she liked insulting me when other people were around because she knew I couldn't argue or discipline her without appearing to be certifiably insane.

"Maybe we just need to look at Bryce a

little closer," I said. "Wasn't there any DNA at the scene? Anything besides Molly's corpse and the hammer? The hammer had to have DNA, right?"

"We're working on it," Trevor replied. "Those things take time."

My phone buzzed in my pocket. I pulled it out to find a text from Erika.

I need my nails done. Can I swing by this afternoon?

There wasn't much afternoon left, but I figured I could squeeze her in between now and dinner. Besides, it gave me the perfect opportunity to discuss the murder with her.

Sure. Can you be at the salon in fifteen?

The little dots formed in the bubble and seconds later, I received a thumbs up.

Your the best, Gina!

With a grimace I set my phone down. I hated improper grammar, even in texts, but I wouldn't be the grammar police to a twenty-something-year-old who wasn't mine. I'd leave that to her own mother.

Did I tell Trevor about my meeting with Erika? It didn't seem important since I was only doing her nails. Sure, I'd bring up Molly's death, but it seemed Erika had already been ruled out as a suspect. Perhaps that was a mistake.

When Trevor pulled up in my driveway, I said, "Be here at six, okay?"

"Yes, ma'am."

"When do you think you'll get everyone's phone records?"

"I'm hoping today," he replied.

"Okay, I'll see you in a bit."

Daisy followed as I exited the car, then bounded up to the front door.

"We're not staying," I said, pulling out my keys. "We're just going to let Marilyn and Frank out, then I have to go do Erika's nails."

"I'll stay here," Daisy said. "I'm going to get Marilyn to play with me."

"Nope. You're coming with me. I don't want a fight between you and Frank, and you seem to be determined to get one."

"I don't want to *fight*," Daisy said. "I want to *play*."

"Please give up on your quest," I sighed. Stuffing my key into the door, I unlocked it and pushed it open. She burst into the living room. "And leave them alone!"

After using the bathroom, I hurried back to the living room to find Daisy running around in circles while the other two stared at her as if she were a funhouse attraction. "Come on, Frank," I said. "Let's get you and Marilyn outside."

They both ran for the back door with Marilyn in the lead, Frank right behind her and Daisy on their heels. Frank glanced behind him every few steps and bared his teeth. I couldn't wait to get rid of these two.

Instead of fighting Daisy to have her stay inside, I let her out with them. She continued to run and try to get Marilyn to play, all to no avail. When she finally trotted to the back door, I opened it.

"It's cold out there," she whined. "I don't like being cold."

"I know."

"If Marilyn would play with me then we'd be warm, and maybe the little tyrant would freeze to death."

"That's not very nice, Daisy."

"And neither is he."

No argument from me. As I waited for Marilyn and Frank to finish their business, I checked my social media. A few people had inquired about them. One woman had two small children, so that wouldn't work. "Why can't people read the description of the perfect house for them?" I muttered, shaking my head. I'd specifically written *no small kids*.

Another post caught my eye from someone named Fiona Wellington.

I just lost my dog. I'd love to look after these two. I live alone and I'm home most of the day. My house is quiet. I'm looking for companionship.

Now, that seemed promising. Of course, I'd have to meet her and make sure her home was what she said it was, but a flicker of hope flared up within my heart.

My two guests came to the back door and I let them in. "Let's go, Daisy!"

I found my dog standing at the front door, her head lowered, her tail almost between her legs. I hated seeing her this sad, but I wasn't sure what to do for her. If I left her, I had no doubt she'd antagonize Frank to the point of a fight. I wished they wanted to play, but they simply weren't interested.

"Come on," I said. "Let's go see Erika."

"Isn't she the one who was at the police station?" Daisy asked before bolting out the front door.

"Yes, she is. She's been in the store many times and you said you liked her."

"I do, I do!" Daisy shouted. "Unless she killed that lady."

"We're going to talk to her about that."

"I hope she didn't do it."

"Me, too."

As we drove into town, I couldn't imagine Erika being so mad about losing her job that she'd beat Molly to death. However, she had deleted the video of her using the pink hammer, and that certainly made her look guilty. At this point, everyone even remotely close to Molly looked guilty to me.

I parked a few spaces down from File It Away to find Erika waiting for me at the door. As Daisy and I exited the car, I watched the woman carefully. She stared at her phone, lifted it as if she was taking a picture and smiled. Then she said something, but I couldn't make it out. Was she filming a video for her TikTok channel?

"Hey, Erika!" I yelled. When she turned, I waved.

"Hi, Gina!" She waited until I was closer, then said, "Thanks for getting me in today."

"Sure." I glanced around. "Did you walk? I don't see your car."

"No. Nick dropped me off and he'll pick me up later. You'll never believe what happened! Hi, Daisy!"

"I can't wait to hear about it." I smiled and unlocked the door.

"Hi, Erika!" Daisy replied, her tail wagging. "You didn't kill anyone, did you? Because if you did, I'm not sure I want you petting me."

After we filed inside, I made a beeline for the thermostat.

"Dang, it's cold in here," Erika said.

"I know. It's been a while since we've been at the store. It'll warm up quickly."

Turning around, I found her seated in a chair. I smiled and hurried over while she slipped out of her boots. Daisy took great interest in them.

"When I pulled up, were you filming for

your TikTok channel?" I asked while turning on the water and waiting for it to get hot.

"No. Nick asked me for a picture, so I sent him one."

I wasn't up on dating, especially among the younger generation, but it seemed weird to send a picture to someone who had dropped her off moments ago. And hadn't I heard her mention they were thinking of living together?

"Didn't you say he just dropped you off?"

"Yes, he did," she replied. "He likes me to check in and send him pictures."

That seemed weird to me. "Why does he want a picture if he just saw you?"

I turned off the water and pointed to it. Erika stuck her feet in. "He loves me and thinks I'm hot."

"That's strange," I muttered.

"You think it's weird my boyfriend thinks I'm hot?" Erika asked.

"No! Oh, no. I didn't mean that. Of course he thinks you're hot. You are." I took a deep breath and tried to correct my wrong. "What's strange to me is that you just saw him and he wants a picture." I shrugged. "We didn't do things like that back in my day."

"You didn't have phones either, right?"

"Yes. For most of my youth, we were phone free, and I feel sorry for you kids who grew up with them."

"I can't imagine my life without it," Erika said while I got started on her toes. "I mean, I can catch up with anyone at any time. I can check in on my boyfriend. I have everything right here at my fingertips!"

"And life was better without it," I grumbled.

While I scrubbed her feet, I glanced up at her nails. Still the same red and green sparkling mess I'd noticed at the police station. Two nails remained broken. Had it happened while she was beating Molly to death? "How did you break your nails?"

"Cleaning," she answered. "I was doing some stuff at the store and they broke off."

"Before Molly died, I assume?"

"Yes, Gina." She rolled her eyes. "I was fired, remember?"

I nodded and concentrated on my work. Erika's phone continued to buzz. Every so often she'd take it out, type something, and shove it back in her pocket.

"So, tell me the good news," I said. I glanced up at her perfectly made-up face. Such a difference from when I'd seen her at the Sheriff's department. Soft blush contoured her dewy cheeks while her eyebrows had been drawn on to perfection. A light pink lipstick coated her plump lips that broke out into a huge grin.

"Well, Lewis called me, and he wants me to come back to the store!"

I smiled. She truly seemed thrilled with the newest development, and I was happy for her. "That's wonderful, Erika. Congratulations."

"Thank you!" she squealed. "Do you see why I need my nails and feet done? I start tomorrow!"

"I understand," I said, returning to her toes. "It's important to make a good impression."

"That's what Nick said. I need to have every hair in place, my clothes ironed and my nails done. I don't want to give Lewis any reason to fire me."

It seemed as though it was the perfect time to question her and see if she had any tidbits regarding Lewis for me. "Did he say if he was bringing in anyone else to help?" I asked.

"Well, he didn't say anything specific, but he did tell me things would be much different."

What did that mean? Would he ease in Debbie, or bring her in from the beginning?

Erika's phone went off again. With a sigh, she pulled it out. A moment later, she snapped a picture of herself smiling, and tapped at the screen.

"Nick again?" I asked. I'd never met the guy and he gave me the creeps.

"Yes." Her brow furrowed as she stared at her phone. "Gina, do my teeth look yellow to you?"

She turned the phone toward me and I studied the picture.

"No. Why?"

"Nick says I need to whiten them."

I pulled off my glasses and squinted at the screen. "Your teeth look fine, and if Nick is picking at you that way, you need to put him in his place."

"What does that mean?" she asked.

"It means that you are a beautiful young woman and if Nick doesn't appreciate you just the way you are, then he needs to go jump in the river."

"He'd freeze to death!"

"That may not be a bad thing," I muttered, slipping on my glasses and getting back to work.

"Gina!"

"Sorry, sorry," I sighed, wishing I'd kept my mouth shut. "I've been through a horrible relationship and I know what a controlling jerk looks like." I shrugged. "Be careful with Nick, okay?"

CHAPTER 15

ERIKA REMAINED quiet the rest of the session, her focus solely on her phone. Daisy had decided she'd had enough of Erika's boots and had gone to her bed. Her soft snores kept us company in between the furnace clicking on and off.

My big mouth may have just lost me a customer, but if it saved Erika from being in an abusive relationship, I was okay with it.

Just as I was finishing up with her hands, the front door opened. I recognized the young man from Erika's videos. He smiled while running a hand through his mop of brown hair. Dressed in a long black trench coat and big black boots, he reminded me of the kids from the goth era of my youth.

"Ready, Erika?" he asked.

"Almost," she said.

"You said you'd be ready now," he replied, his grin fading.

I stood and smiled, then walked over to him. "You must be Nick," I said, hoping the fact I was seething inside didn't show. "I'm Gina." I stuck out my hand and he shook it. "I've heard a lot about you."

He nodded, then glanced over my shoulder at Erika. "Let's go."

"She's not ready yet because of me," I said, stepping into his view once again and pointing to a chair by the front door. "You can take a seat right there and I'll let you know when we're done."

He rolled his eyes and sighed. "We've got to go. She told me she'd be ready now, and I'm here. So she can get up *right now*."

I took a step toward him and lowered my voice. At five foot three I wasn't a very imposing figure, but hopefully my message would come across loud and clear. "I know men like you all too well, you ignorant bully.

Sit. Down. Erika will leave when I'm finished and not before."

He glared at me for a long moment, then did as I had suggested. I hurried back to Erika, hoping I hadn't made her life more difficult. She needed to get away from him, and the sooner the better.

I smiled as I settled back on the seat and started with her nails. She'd chosen sky blue and requested rhinestones in a rainbow shape across them. Silence once again blanketed the studio. Even Daisy had woken and didn't take her stare off Nick. After a moment, he stood and began to pace. I ignored him, but I noted Erika kept glancing over to him as if she were worried.

A few minutes later, I announced, "All done. Let me help you get your boots on, and then you're free to leave."

"Thanks a lot, Gina," she said. "I appreciate you fitting me in."

"Anything for you, Erika." I retrieved her boots and helped her slip them on while she placed her nails under the dryer. "Don't allow him to push you around," I whispered.

"He only wants what's best for me," she muttered. "He loves me."

I wound up a speech about how love wasn't controlling and picking apart someone's looks, but then I glanced over at Nick and decided to hold it. I certainly didn't want to poke the bear and have Erika suffer the consequences.

After she paid, Nick grabbed her arm and pulled her outside. I didn't turn around, but heard them.

"Why did you get blue?" he asked.

"You told me to!"

"I told you to get midnight blue, not this baby blue!" His language became more colorful as he berated her choice.

"They are fighting," Daisy said as she trotted to the door. "Erika looks so sad."

"I should mind my own business," I muttered.

"You should go punch him in the face," Daisy corrected.

She always gave me the best / worst ideas. So I hurried outside and pushed Nick away from Erika. "She can paint her nails any dang color she wants. Leave her alone!"

"Gina!" Erika shouted. "Stop it!"

I turned to her and she shook her head, then stomped away with tears in her eyes. "You need to be nicer to her," I said as I faced Nick. "Stop nitpicking her."

"I want the best for her!" he said, raising his arms to his sides. "Her hands look better with a darker polish! I love her, and I want her to be happy."

"Then quit hassling her about how white her teeth are and the color she chose for her nails!"

"I'd do anything for that woman," he growled placing his face inches from mine. "I want her happy. Now, if you'll excuse me, I have to go make my girlfriend smile because you've stuck your nose where it doesn't belong."

As he ran to catch up to Erika, his black trench coat flew behind him like a villains' cape. I crossed my arms over my chest and shivered. He threw his arm around her shoulder and pulled her close. Maybe I was wrong. Maybe I didn't know a thing about healthy relationships since I'd never been in one.

I turned and noticed Daisy with her nose against the window leaving streaks for me to clean at some point in the near future. I'd asked her at least a thousand times not to do that, but it fell on deaf ears. As I stepped inside, she wagged her tail.

"Are we done for the day?" she asked.

I nodded and walked over to sanitize the bowl I'd used for Erika.

"She wasn't happy with you, Gina."

"I know. Like my brother said, if I just minded my own business, my life would be easier."

"Maybe, maybe not. But let's go home! Trevor's coming over, right?"

I groaned as I scrubbed the bowl. The last thing I wanted was company.

"Yay, Trevor!" she yelled while spinning around in a circle. "I love Trevor! You should marry him so he can pet me all the time!"

With a snort, I shook my head. Me being married was about as ridiculous as me giving out relationship advice to a twenty-something-year-old woman. It was on the list of things the universe shouldn't allow to happen.

I glanced at the clock. Trevor would be arriving at my house shortly. Suddenly, I became bone tired and had no desire to cook. However, I did owe him since he hadn't busted me for my felony.

"Do you think breakfast burritos from On The River would be okay to serve?" I asked.

"You told him steak," Daisy replied. "And I was looking forward to the leftovers. You'll disappoint both of us."

"Fine." I grumbled a curse, stood, then hurried over to the door to fetch my coat. "Let's go."

When we arrived home, Trevor was waiting for us in the driveway. Daisy leapt from the car and jumped and danced around him all while shouting his name. I wished she'd be that excited to see me.

"I've got great news," Trevor said as he followed me to the door while trying not to step on Daisy as she bounced at his feet.

"Good. I could use some."

"Bad afternoon?"

I unlocked the door and pushed it open.

"I don't know if I'm just getting old or young people are dumb."

He shrugged and grinned. "Maybe a bit of both?"

"Thanks," I said, shucking my coat. "Do you want a beer?"

"That would be great."

After pouring myself a glass of wine and fetching Trevor a bottle, I settled down on the couch while he plopped down on the other side. Daisy jumped up between us and stretched out, placed her head on Trevor's lap and gazed up at him lovingly, completely ignoring Frank and Marilyn who lay in the corner of the living room, eyeing us warily.

I couldn't believe the amount of hair coming off Marilyn. There were furballs floating around everywhere. I needed to take a vacuum to the floor and a brush to the dog.

Daisy began to giggle, then glanced over at me. A moment later, I smelled her gas and almost choked on my wine. "You're so gross," I muttered, waving my hand in front of my face.

It was so bad, even Trevor grimaced while

Daisy continued to find her own antics quite funny.

"This tastes good," Trevor said after taking a long gulp, then pointed at Frank and Marilyn. "Those two aren't very social."

"No, they prefer to keep to themselves."

"They're meanie weenies," Daisy pouted.

I stroked her head while asking Trevor, "So, what's your big news?"

"I've got Lewis nailed," he said, grinning. "I just need a few more pieces of evidence, but he's the killer."

I sat stunned. "What... how did you figure it out?"

"Phone records," he said. "I finally got them. Lewis lied. He was at the store that night. His location service pings him there at the time of Molly's murder."

My mouth fell open and I gaped at him for a moment. "You've got to be kidding me."

"Nope. I'm just waiting on the DNA from the crime scene, and then that will be it. I'll have all the ducks in a row to arrest him. He's got motive—his wife was leaving him and he knew she'd take half of everything. If he got rid of her, he'd have his store, his house and Debbie. He was at the store that night and he's bigger than Molly, so killing her with a hammer isn't that big of a stretch. It's him, Gina."

I considered Erika's account of what she'd seen that night when she returned to the store to beg for her job back. She hadn't been sure, but she'd thought she'd saw a man standing at the end of the dark hallway. Could it have been Lewis, waiting for her to leave before he bludgeoned his wife to death?

It all made sense, but for some reason, it didn't sit well with me. "Are you sure about it, Trevor?"

"Yep." He took another sip of beer. "Looking forward to getting this one closed."

"Hey, Gina?" Daisy said.

"Okay, well, I guess congratulations are in order," I said. "I'll get the steaks ready."

"How about we just call for a pizza?" Trevor asked. "My treat."

"I won't argue with that." Thank goodness I didn't have to cook.

Trevor pulled out his phone and dialed, then walked into the kitchen. As he ordered a pepperoni pizza and some mozzarella sticks, he opened the refrigerator door. Fetching another beer would be my guess. Daisy stood and turned around so we were face to face.

"Gina? I have something to tell you, and I have a feeling you're going to be really mad at me."

I arched an eyebrow. Usually, when she started a conversation like that, yes, I did end up mad. But it was always something about how she couldn't help herself when she dug a hole in the backyard, or how that sock had jumped into her mouth, so she had to rip it to pieces. "What's that?" I sighed.

"When Erika was in the store today, I think I smelled blood on her boots."

CHAPTER 16

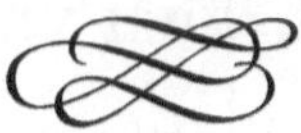

"Wʜᴀᴛ?!" I hissed. "Why didn't you tell me this earlier?!"

"I was going to after Erika left, but then Nick arrived and he was such a jerk I forgot. Then Trevor came over and I got really excited and then when you two started talking about everything, I remembered."

"Whose blood was it?" I whispered, glancing at the kitchen. Thankfully, the person on the other line was having trouble getting Trevor's order right. For the third time, he repeated it. It bought me a few moments for this explosive conversation.

"I don't know if it even was blood," she

scoffed. "It kind of smelled like it, though. I'm not a vampire."

"Was it human? Or maybe an animal?"

"Gina, I don't know any of that. I may have smelled blood. That's all I can tell you."

With a sigh, I glanced around the living room, wishing she'd shared this information with me earlier. My interaction with Erika could've been a lot different. First, I would've studied her boots for the stains. They'd been black, so I wouldn't have noticed any discoloration on them unless I'd been looking for it.

I would have also asked more questions about her whereabouts the night Molly was murdered, not to mention I would've dived further into Lewis and Molly's relationship. Certainly, I wouldn't have spent so much time focusing on her loser boyfriend.

Could Daisy match up the scent of Erika's boots to the blood from the crime scene? And how in the world could I make that happen? Lewis had cleaned the store, but there'd be bits of evidence he wouldn't be able to see or find. Perhaps Daisy could, though. He had a firm no dogs in the store policy, but maybe I could swing by when he wasn't there? Erika had allowed me in with Daisy once or twice before when her boss was gone.

But wait... Erika could've stepped in it anywhere—if it even was really blood. Just because she may have had blood on her shoe didn't mean she'd killed Molly. Heck, maybe someone had a bloody nose while walking around downtown and she'd accidentally walked right through it, none the wiser.

Although, she was quite upset that she'd lost her job and now she had it back, and she'd admitted she *had been* there that night.

The worst part was that Trevor was convinced it was Lewis... unless Erika and Lewis were in on it together. He'd get his wife out of the way, he'd retain full control of the store and his money, and Erika would get her job back. Wouldn't that be a heck of a twist?

Then there was Geoff. Something felt off when we'd spoken to him. And money was a great motivator to kill. Trevor hadn't mentioned anything about his phone records.

I took a long slug of wine. It wouldn't help me think any clearer, but it sure tasted good.

As Daisy lay back down, Trevor walked

into the living room. "New girl at the pizza place," he said. "She needs a lot more training." He sat down and sighed, then sipped his beer. "It should be here in about twenty minutes."

I nodded and pursed my lips. "Trevor, I have a question."

He turned to face me. "What's that?"

"Well, actually, I have a few of them."

"Hit me with all of them." He chuckled.

"What did Geoff's phone records show?"

"He was at home. I've pretty much ruled him out."

I couldn't, though.

"How do you know that Bryce actually went hunting? Did you see the deer he claimed to have killed?"

Trevor's brow furrowed as his smile faded. "No."

"He could've snapped, Trevor. Molly could've told him they were done and their plans of her bringing money into his life may have been the straw that broke the camel's back, so to speak."

"It's possible."

"And what about Erika?" Goodness, I felt

so ugly with her name leaving my lips in this conversation. "She had just gotten fired. She went back to the store and begged for her job. What if she lost control of her anger?"

"We don't have any evidence of it," he said. "Besides, her phone records indicate that she was home that night."

And she may have blood on her boots!

I shrugged. "Who takes their phone to a murder? If she is smart, and she is, she'd leave it at home with location turned on for an alibi. Same with Geoff."

"You were so certain earlier that Erika was innocent," Trevor commented.

And that was the problem. I couldn't tell him my talking dog had just given me crucial information while he was ordering a pizza. Reaching over, I stroked Daisy's head. "I've just been thinking about it. It seems there's a lot of evidence pointing to her. First, the video on TikTok with her expertly wielding the pink hammer, which has now been deleted. She had broken fingernails when I saw her the morning after the murder at the Sheriff's department. When I asked her about it today, she said she broke them cleaning at

Hammer and Nail. I can't imagine what type of cleaning would snap two nails like that. Were there any fake nails found at the store?"

He nodded. "There was one found on the next aisle over from the crime scene. It was green and red. Christmassy."

"Those are the colors she had when Molly was murdered. I did them myself. When they snap off, they can travel pretty far. Or it could've been kicked over there while in the heat of the killing."

As the color drained from his face, I continued, even though I wanted to vomit. There was a lot of evidence against Erika, but I didn't want it to look like I was zeroing in on her, although it seemed to me that Trevor should. Instead, I brought up other unanswered questions I had, hoping for answers that would clear the other suspects and show him that he needed to focus on Erika without actually bringing up the fact my dog may have smelled blood on her shoes. "And let's not forget Debbie. She's as paranoid as they come about people discovering her affair with Lewis. He'd told her many times he was leaving and he never did. What if she got

Molly out of the way herself? She's slid into her new role easily and quickly."

"That's true," Trevor said. "But I have Lewis' phone at the store at the time of death, Gina. No one else checks out like that."

"Well, as I mentioned, I wouldn't take a phone to a murder I planned."

Trevor shrugged. "Maybe he didn't plan it. Maybe he killed her in the heat of the moment during a fight."

"Maybe," I sighed.

"You're totally bringing me down, Gina. Here I thought I had everything lined up, but you've asked some questions I can't answer."

"I know, and I'm sorry. I hate to say it, but you need to take a second look at Erika," I said quietly. "It seems a lot of evidence points to her."

"Except her phone records. She was at home."

"She probably has blood on her boots!" Daisy yelled.

We sat in silence for a long while. When the doorbell rang, it startled all of us, sending the three dogs into a cacophony of barking. Marilyn jumped up and ran for the door with

Frank literally nipping at her heels as if he was mad she was in front of him.

"I'll get it," Trevor said, standing.

"I'll hold the vicious canines back," I muttered, also rising from the couch.

Once the pizza was collected, we sat back down. Daisy put her nose right up to the box while Marilyn and Frank watched from afar.

"Get out of here," I said, tapping her snout. "Don't be so rude."

"Well, *if you'd feed me*, Gina, then maybe I wouldn't be so hungry!"

I narrowed my gaze at her for a long moment, trying to remember if I fed the dogs when I arrived home. Sometimes she said I hadn't when I actually had, just to get a few more treats.

No, I'd neglected to feed the dogs. "I forgot to put their bowls out," I muttered. Standing, I went to the kitchen while swearing under my breath.

I placed Frank and Marilyn's bowls by the oven and brought Daisy's into the living room so I could keep an eye on her, then I sat down to dive into the pizza.

After a while, Trevor said, "You know,

Gina, I think we really need to talk about your mom."

Heck, no, we don't.

I held up my hand. "No."

I'd done an excellent job at putting that out of my mind. I didn't want to know anything about her at this point.

"Gina—"

"No, Trevor." I sighed and shoved the last bit of pizza in my mouth. "Didn't you order pepperoni?"

"Yes. They brought sausage, though."

"That girl at the pizza place really does need more training."

"The information I have about your mom is important," he said gently. "Quit trying to change the subject."

"Not now," I said quietly. "I can't deal with it now."

"Okay." He shrugged. "It's your call. You let me know when."

We ate in silence while I pushed all thoughts of Brandy Dunner aside. There wasn't any curiosity about what Trevor may have to say, only stark fear. I didn't want to know.

After Trevor left, I decided to get work done on my ghostwriting project. I added in some of the more recent details and wondered how it all fit together. Who had killed Molly? Or in the case of my book, Paulina, the name I'd given the victim.

As I stared at my screen, I decided to return to my notebook where I'd written down everything I felt needed to be done to find the killer. I picked it up and stared at the page. The phone records were in. Debbie had adopted a kitten. We still didn't know who the man Erika had seen in the hallway was, if there'd been one. Trevor said Geoff was in the clear because he'd been home—same with Bryce. But had he really gone hunting?

And what about Wanda? She had a fire in her, but was it strong enough to kill the woman who owed her and her husband money?

"Even with all these questions, everything still comes back to Erika," I said out loud.

"You should just call her Bloody Boots from now on," Daisy replied from the bed. "She's a murderer. A very bad dog."

I snorted and nodded my head. "You said you didn't know if that was blood for sure."

"Let's pretend it is," she replied. "Then you can throw her in jail and get those two dummies in the living room adopted so I can go back to having a fun life."

"I can't just get someone arrested so your life becomes a bit easier, Daisy."

"All the evidence points to her, Gina," Daisy said. "You have to go to where your sniffer takes you."

Placing my notebook to the side, I worked on my manuscript for a little while longer and became so engaged, I didn't realize Daisy had left the room until I heard growling down the hall.

With a curse, I hurried to the living room. Daisy and Frank were in a standoff, both baring their teeth, while Marilyn stood behind the tiny brown sausage.

"Knock it off!" I yelled.

Neither moved.

"Enough!" I stepped between them. To my shock, Frank ran around me and attacked Daisy. The two wrestled on the carpet for a few seconds with teeth snapping and both growling until I was able to grab Daisy's collar and pull her off. Frank lunged again, and I grabbed his collar as well. Holding them both apart, I snapped, "Daisy, you need to go into the bedroom, right now. I'm very disappointed in your behavior."

"Let go of me, Gina!"

"Go. To. The. Bedroom."

"Fine." I let go of her. "Tell him that Marilyn isn't all his and she can do what she wants. I tried, but the little wiener won't listen!" She growled again, then I yelled and pointed to the bedroom.

After she trotted down the hall, I released Frank. The little jerk ran back over to Marilyn and licked her face. Why in the world wouldn't he allow Marilyn to play with Daisy? Was it love? Or was it control?

I took a deep breath and sank to my knees in front of the two, wishing I could have conversations with them like I did with Daisy. As I reached out to pet Marilyn, Frank bared his teeth. "Don't you pull that with me," I hissed.

I slowly laid my hand on his head, then reached for Marilyn again. This time, he allowed me to touch her.

He was so protective of her, and it seemed like he'd do anything to make sure she was well and safe. Instead, he smothered her while not allowing her to make her own decisions.

My heart thundered as I stroked the two dogs. Was I seeing things that weren't there, or had Marilyn and Frank just revealed the killer to me?

And if so, how in the world did I prove it?

CHAPTER 17

I TOSSED and turned all night, trying to figure out if I was losing my mind or if the dogs had solved this murder for me. Could Nick have killed because he loved Erika so much and he didn't like to see her upset?

In the morning as I drank my coffee, I decided there was only one way to find out. I had to threaten Erika in some way and see how Nick responded. I wasn't looking forward to baiting him like that, but I needed to know if I was right.

Every time I tried to invent a way to instigate my plan, I kept returning to the idea that I needed Annabelle's help. She was a master at planning and conniving, mainly to get revenge on those who had hurt her or those she cared about.

For instance, when my ex-husband had been killed and we discovered he had thousands and thousands of dollars hidden in his walls, she'd broken in and stolen ten thousand dollars for me. I'd almost felt guilty for taking the money, but the deadbeat hadn't paid me child support while I raised my son, so I used it to help send Jacob to college.

When our friend Jordan had ended his relationship with our friend Sam, Annabelle had broken into his house and put saran wrap around his toilet. She'd slashed tires and put laxative in chocolates. Her creativity was unsurpassed, and I needed help.

I texted her and asked if we could meet at the local coffee shop, Cup of Go, and she readily agreed.

Without explanation, I told Daisy I would be locking her in the bedroom. "I can't trust you to be around Frank and Marilyn while I'm out."

"You could take me with you," she said

hopefully. "I am a creature of God, you know."

"Yes, yes," I sighed. "You've mentioned that. For now, you'll need to stay home."

"That's too bad because I could be a big help."

Pursing my lips, I sighed. If it were up to me, the world would be wide open to dogs, but unfortunately, I wasn't in charge. Instead, I gave her an extra treat and said my goodbyes.

I arrived at Cup of Go a few minutes early and ordered Annabelle a cappuccino and an Americano with heavy cream for myself. The pastries looked amazing, so I also picked up a couple of chocolate scones for us, then found a table by the window, tucked away in a corner. Below me, the cold river meandered by. On the other bank sat miles of forest. In the summer, Heywood became a tourist hub full of people river rafting. I preferred the quiet of winter, despite hating the frigid temperatures.

Annabelle sashayed into the coffee shop wearing her neon pink floor-length parka with a matching hat and gloves and black boots. Over her shoulder was a large black bag featuring a young Axl Rose and the Guns and Roses logo. As our gazes met, she smiled.

"You look like a mascot for Pepto Bissell," I said, standing to hug her.

As she giggled, she took me into an embrace, and I fought the predictable desire to bristle at her touch. "You'll never, ever look as cute as me, Gina Dunner."

She shucked her coat before sitting down to reveal a neon green turtleneck and a black Duran Duran t-shirt over it. She tossed her crimped, blonde hair over her shoulder and smiled. "Thank you for my coffee."

"I also got you a scone." I pushed the plate toward her and she narrowed her gaze.

"Hmm... you're being way too nice. What do you want from me?"

As she took a bite from the pastry, I sighed. Was I really that transparent? "Well, I wanted to talk to you about Molly Burton's murder and have you tell me if I'm crazy or not. And if you don't think I am, then I need your help."

She smiled and nodded. "I almost didn't come. I was going to, like, make an excuse. I'm so glad I didn't. Tell me everything."

"Okay, so—"

"Have you said anything to Trevor about this?"

I shook my head.

She squealed and grinned. "Coolness. Even better. I like being first in the know. Go on."

Glancing around, I made sure no one was listening in. The coast was clear, so I continued. "When Molly was killed, we all thought that maybe Lewis had something to do with it. Remember?"

"Yes, because he was having an affair and wanted Molly gone."

"Right. And she had also taken a great interest in the store, so we considered she was going to divorce him and take half of everything."

"And I heard that Molly was having an affair as well," Annabelle said.

"Yes. His name's Bryce. I don't think he had anything to do with it."

"I don't think so either," Annabelle sniffed. "If he really wanted Molly all to himself, he would've killed Lewis."

I sat back in my chair and stared at my friend. That was an angle I hadn't considered.

"What if Molly had kicked him to the curb and he wasn't happy about it? Then he could be the killer."

"Well, that's true." She furrowed her brow and tapped the side of her cup. "That would make him a good suspect."

"Agreed, but I still don't think he did it."

She leaned over the table, her eyes wide. "Who do you think it was?"

"I'm not going to lie. All the evidence points to Erika."

"Really? Like what?"

I explained about the deleted video and her being at the store that night, but I had to fudge about the rest. "I thought I saw blood on her boots when she was in getting her mani / pedi."

"Did you, like, ask her about it?"

"No. I didn't know how to bring it up without being accusatory."

Annabelle snorted and rolled her eyes. "If she killed someone, then you can be as accusatory as you want."

"I was in shock," I said.

"That's never stopped you from saying what's on your mind."

She apparently wasn't buying my lies, so I moved on.

"Anyway, there was a dog fight at my house last night."

"How did we move from murder to dogs?" Annabelle lifted her cup and stared at me over the brim.

"I know it's a jump, but listen. I took in these rescues. They're a bonded pair and the little one is very protective of the big one. He doesn't want Daisy or me near her, but Daisy keeps pushing him, trying to get the other one to play. When I broke up a fight last night between Daisy and him, it occurred to me that Erika's relationship with her boyfriend, Nick, is a lot like the dogs' relationship. Based on what she's told me, what I've witnessed for myself and what she's posted on TikTok, he's very protective of her."

"I've seen it," Annabelle said. "She just started coming to me for her skincare because Nick said her complexion isn't smooth enough and claims some of the products she uses are toxic."

With a sigh, I shook my head. "See what I mean?"

"I do. She's got beautiful skin, but he's right. The products she uses are horrible. Did you know there are over a thousand ingredients that the United States allows in their personal care products that are banned in Europe? We have to be *so* careful, Gina. We live in, like, a toxic soup and don't even realize it."

Ugh. I knew the pharmaceutical industry was bad enough, but I had no idea the corruption had slithered into personal products. "Maybe I need to bring in my skincare line to you and have you look at it."

Annabelle nodded in agreement. "You should."

My skincare was quite minimal, but it would be a good idea to get her feedback.

First though, I needed to solve a murder.

"Anyway, he doesn't like her spending much time talking to men. He was at my store yesterday, mad because she wasn't ready when she said she was going to be. He's just... he's a controlling jerk."

"So why do you think he killed Molly?" Annabelle asked.

"Because Molly upset Erika," I said. "Erika told me she went back to beg for her job, then she went home. While there, she said she thought she may have seen a man at the end of the hallway, but she wasn't sure. What if that was Nick, waiting to see if she got her job back?"

Annabelle gasped. "Then when she didn't, he killed Molly?"

"Exactly. Erika said she called Molly some pretty horrible names and said things she shouldn't have. If Nick had been lying in wait, then he'd have heard all of it and realized just how upset Erika was at being fired."

"And being the knight in shining armor he is, he had to do something about it."

"There's a fine line between being a knight in shining armor and a controlling psy-chopath."

Annabelle nodded. "That's, like, totally true."

"So, what do you think?" I asked. "Do you think I'm crazy? Am I seeing things that aren't there?"

She furrowed her brow as she devoured the rest of her scone. "I don't know. Who does Trevor think killed her?"

"Lewis. His phone was at Hammer and Nail at the time of Molly's murder."

"That's kind of a good clue."

"Would you bring your phone to a murder?" I asked.

"Of course not. That would be, like, totally stupid."

I shrugged. "Exactly my point."

Annabelle stared out the window for a long moment. "I don't think you're crazy," she said as she met my gaze. "There's a good possibility that Nick killed Molly. It's iffy, but if he's a psycho, then it makes sense in his head."

With a sigh of relief, I smiled. "Thank you."

"So what are you going to do about it?" she asked.

"I was hoping you could help me set a trap for him."

Annabelle's eyes lit up as if I'd just handed her a million dollars. "Oh, my goodness," she whispered. "This day just keeps getting better and better. First, my hair looks extra cute. Then you text me for coffee, and now this." She shook her head.

"So, you'll help me?"

"Of course."

"We can't let Erika know about any plan," I said. "She's too enthralled with him. She may have some doubts about her relationship, but they aren't strong enough to try to pin a murder on him."

"Understandable. We want to elicit the same response from him that Erika getting fired did. So, somehow, we need to hurt Erika."

You're right," I agreed. "The issue is going to be to find something that upsets Erika but doesn't physically injure her, just like the firing did."

We spent an hour devising a plan, and frankly, I felt a little bad about going behind Erika's back to trap her loser boyfriend. However, if I didn't, someone innocent may go to jail.

A few of the things Annabelle suggested —like taking her prisoner and leaving clues for Nick on where he could find her—I quickly nixed. The last thing we needed was to be arrested for kidnapping or killed by Nick for doing so.

Instead, we devised a plan that I felt would work. At least it would poke the beast and we could see what his response would be.

"What is Doug going to say about this?" I asked.

"Nothing. He was invited to speak to a rehab group in Phoenix, so he's out of town for a few days. I'm so proud of him and how far he's come."

"That's amazing," I said. "I'm happy for him."

"Thanks."

Silence fell over the table for a moment as I considered grabbing another coffee if we were going to continue our conversation, but then Annabelle said, "I've got to get back to Sage Advice. Let's put our plan into action either this afternoon or tomorrow."

Nervous butterflies tickled my stomach. "You're going to call her?"

"Yes."

"I don't like putting you in danger, Annabelle," I said.

"Don't worry about me, Gina." She tapped the side of her Guns n' Roses bag, which happened to be Axl Roses' nose. "I've always got my gun with me. If Nick comes at me, he's either going to end up arrested or dead."

CHAPTER 18

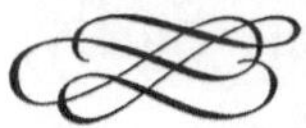

I SPENT the next few hours trying not to think about my plan with Annabelle. Everything rested on her not giving it away and playing everything just right. I prayed Erika never found about our involvement to trap her boyfriend and hopefully send him away for murder.

Instead, I locked myself and Daisy in the bedroom and called Fiona Wellington, the woman who'd expressed interest in adopting Frank and Marilyn. She had moved to the States forty years ago to be with a young man who would later become her husband. She'd met him when he was touring Europe—he'd stopped in the bakery she'd worked in to grab a pastry. She said it had been love at first sight, and it sounded a bit like one of those Hallmark movies to me, which weren't my favorites. But, I was really happy it had all worked out for her. Sadly, he'd passed away this year, as had her dog. "I'm lonely," she said. "I would love the company, but I also don't like dogs that insist on being fussed over."

"These two fuss over each other, not humans," I replied. "They may grow to love you, but I don't think they're needy."

"They sound perfect. I'd love to meet them," she said, her British accent still thick, even after forty years in the States.

We set up a date and time for me to bring them to her house the next day, and I was hopeful. My only concern was her age. If she left Europe in her twenties, that would put her somewhere in her sixties, or even possibly older if she came to the States at a later age. Although Frank and Marilyn were fairly self-sufficient, they did require some level of care. I hoped that Fiona was a very healthy sixty-something-year-old so the dogs would have the opportunity to grow old at her home.

I also spent some time writing my mystery novel, including typing out the scene where my character catches the killer. "I sure hope it works out as good as I wrote it," I said to my sleeping dog.

During all of this, I checked my phone consistently in case I missed Annabelle's call. Considering I had my phone on in my pocket with the volume as high as it could go, it shouldn't have been a worry, but I found myself checking anyway.

"I'm bored," Daisy said from the bed. "You have me locked up in this bedroom like I'm the bad dog."

"Well, you kind of are," I muttered. "If you'd leave Marilyn and Frank alone, I wouldn't have to contain you."

"I don't like Frank."

"You've made that very clear."

"But Marilyn does," she continued. "He won't let her play and she still likes him. Why is that, Gina?"

I wish I had an answer. It was a typical abusive, controlling relationship, one that baffled me in humans, and I certainly couldn't explain in a dog's view. "I don't understand it either. But it's the way it is, so we need to get through the day. Hopefully, they'll be gone tomorrow."

"I hope so," Daisy grumbled. "Because I'm bored."

"We may be going to see Annabelle to-day," I said. "You'll come with me and see Jack."

"Oh, yay! When do we leave, Gina?" She stood and ran around in circles on my bed. "Jack will play with me!"

"We'll leave if she calls. For now, you need to settle down."

"Fine," she huffed. "I'll be a good dog."

A few moments later, my phone rang and just about scared me to death it was so loud. Daisy began to bark and I shushed her before answering.

"Did you talk to her?" I asked.

"Yes," Annabelle whispered. "She'll be here at two."

I lowered my voice as well. "Do you think it'll work?"

"Of course it will," she said. "It's the per-fect plan, Gina. If Nick is the loser we think he is, he'll take the bait."

"Okay." I rubbed my sweaty palm on my jeans. "I'm really nervous."

"Just get over here. It's going to be fine. You don't have to do anything but, like, sit in the back room. I'll take care of it all."

"Why are we whispering?" I asked.

"Because we're about to bait a murderer and I don't want anyone to hear my plan. Get over here."

I set my phone down and took a deep breath. We were really going through with it.

"I think this may be a bad idea," I said.

"I don't even know what your idea is, but if Annabelle helped you with it, it's probably terrible," Daisy replied.

Pursing my lips, I considered her statement. Was she right? Most likely. Should I call Annabelle back and hit the brakes on our trap?

We didn't have a backup plan, so we had to move forward with this one. Especially since Trevor was pretty intent on nailing Lewis for the killing. Hopefully I'd bought Lewis some time before Trevor arrested him by pointing him in Erika's direction. Well, I'd thrown a lot of different scenarios at him and given him a lot to think about, even though the most damning evidence pointed to Lewis—his phone being at the store at the time of the murder.

"Okay, let's go," I said.

After retrieving my coat and leashing Daisy, I said goodbye to Frank and Marilyn. They stared at me from the couch for a brief second, then laid their heads down.

"Bye, jerks," Daisy called. "I get to go out and you don't. I'm going to play with my friend Jack, who wouldn't like you either."

"Daisy," I hissed. "Come on. Stop it." I couldn't wait for my visitors to leave.

We drove to town. I couldn't park in front of Sage Advice in case Erika recognized my car. Instead, I drove up the road a bit and settled for the church parking lot. Unless she came to pray, she'd never see it.

After leashing Daisy, we hurried back down the road and into Sage Advice. I unleashed her and she ran straight to the back, yelling for her friend. Annabelle weaved her way through the display tables, grabbed my arm and dragged me past the cash register and into the back room.

"Okay, here's the deal," she said. No hugs, no witty banter. Just getting down to business. I liked this side of my friend. "I'm going to deal with Erika out front. You just need to stay put."

"That's my job? Staying put?"

She shook her head. "You're my backup, Gina. If things are going bad and I feel I need you, I'm going to yell *avocado*."

I rolled my eyes. "Why not just yell for me?"

"What if she starts talking about you for some reason?" She placed her hands on her hips and sighed, as if I were the stupidest person she'd run into that day. "Then I, like, say your name and you come running out and the whole plan is ruined because I can't explain why you're hiding out in my store!"

"Got it," I replied. "I understand."

"So what's the word?"

"Avocado."

"Perfect." She glanced at the clock on the wall. "She should be here soon. I've told her I've got a new concoction that will help close her pores. She's excited, so she won't miss the appointment."

"It won't hurt her, right?" I was truly worried about Erika being injured.

Annabelle waved her hand in front of her face. "Of course not. It'll be fine."

"My guess is Nick will bring her here, leave and then pick her up," I said.

"I agree. That's what has happened every time she's been here."

"Do you think he won't let her drive her own car, or that she prefers to be shuttled around?"

"I don't know," Annabelle shrugged. "I supposed I could ask her. Just kind of, like, slip it into the conversation."

"And you think he'll come back later tonight to do you in for what you did to Erika, right?"

"If he's the killer, then yes. I'm going to make her life miserable for a couple of hours. The way he's focused on her looks and how controlling he is... he's going to be mad, she's going to be mad, and I can, like, see him getting revenge for her, just like he did when Molly fired Erika."

We sat in the back room for the next hour. Annabelle drank some tea in between waiting on customers, the dogs ran up and down the staircase chasing each other, and I went stir crazy. Being idle was not in my character.

As the clock crawled closer to two, I began to pace. At five minutes until the top of the hour, the door chimes rang and Annabelle winked at me, put a smile on her face, and headed to the front of the store. "Erika!" she called. "Thanks for coming in today! Hi, Nick!"

We'd been right about Erika's arrival. To me, having her boyfriend drive her everywhere was very controlling—especially when he was doing it in her car.

The dogs came barreling down the stairs and out into the store. In a moment of horror, I realized my dog was about to give away that I was there.

"Is that Daisy?" Erika asked.

"Hi, Erika!" Daisy yelled. "You should run! The humans are being bad dogs!"

"It is," Annabelle said. "I'm watching her for a few hours while Gina attends to some business." My shoulders sagged in relief. Thankfully, Annabelle was quick thinking and expert liar. "Let's get started. Nick, are you staying?"

"How long do you think you'll be?" he asked.

"Maybe a half-hour or so?" Annabelle replied.

"I'll be back then. Bye, babe."

The door chimes sounded again, indicating his departure.

"Okay, let's take a look at you," Annabelle said softly. "I appreciate you coming in with a fresh, make-up free face."

I shut my eyes, wishing we'd never started this plan. Erika was a vulnerable young woman and I felt ugly taking advantage of that attribute. However, I was certain her boyfriend had killed Molly, and he needed to pay for that. If she got away from him, it would be good for her, as well. But it wouldn't be an easy separation. She was in deep and unable to see the controlling jerk for what he was, to realize what a horrible situation she was in. *We're doing her a favor.*

"So, your pores are looking a little better than last time," Annabelle said. "But I'd like to see if we can speed up their closure a bit with this new concoction I've made."

"Sure. That would be great."

"Like I said, it's new, and I've made it very powerful. I'd like to test it on your arm before I start slathering it all over your face."

"Okay, Annabelle."

I sank to the floor and leaned against the wall. Making it to a stool seemed like too much effort. Besides, I was right by the doorway and could hear everything if I stayed put.

"Here we go, then," Annabelle said. "What are your plans for the rest of the day?"

As the two discussed how happy Erika was about her morning shift at Hammer and Nail Hardware, and then moved on to the evening plans of Nick taking her out to dinner, I tuned them out for a bit. Mundane small talk always bored me.

Daisy came in and licked my face. "What are you doing, Gina?"

I brought my finger to my mouth, hoping she'd get the point that I couldn't speak.

"I'm not sure what's going on here, but I can tell this is a bad idea."

No argument from me. I was regretting it more and more with every second.

When Jack raced up the stairs as fast as he could, Daisy glanced over her shoulder. "Jack is so much fun to play with," she said. "Bye, Gina!"

While she followed, I listened in to the conversation again.

"I think we can put some on your face now," Annabelle said. "Just shut your eyes." A moment later she asked, "How come Nick, like, drives you everywhere? Are you afraid to drive in the snow?"

"No. I've lived here long enough that snow doesn't bother me. You know, Annabelle, my arm is feeling—"

"Then why don't you drive yourself?" Annabelle interrupted.

"Nick likes to drive, so I let him. My arm... I think I may be having a reaction."

"It looks okay," Annabelle replied. "What do you, like, feel?"

"My arm's warm."

"Well, let's get it washed off."

"Get this stuff off my face first!" Erika yelled loudly.

"Hang on. I'm almost done with your arm."

"Annabelle!"

"It's okay, Erika. Just relax. I'm working as fast as I can to clean it."

"Give me a mirror."

"Well, I can say that you're having a reaction."

"Look at my arm, Annabelle!" she yelled. "Get me a mirror! Does my face look like that?"

"It's not that bad," Annabelle said, her voice calm. "I have some salve that will heal it quickly."

The door chimed again, just as Erika began sobbing. My gut twisted with guilt.

"What the heck is going on here?" Nick's voice boomed. "Erika, what's wrong with your dang face?"

CHAPTER 19

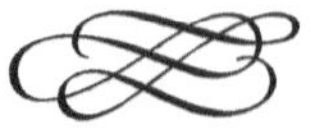

"WHAT HAVE YOU DONE TO ME?!" Erika wailed, and I shut my eyes. Poor thing.

Nick cursed at Annabelle.

"You don't need to speak to me like that!" she replied.

"Yes, I do! My girlfriend's face has red welts on it! How in the world am I supposed to be seen with her looking like that?!"

Erika wailed louder while I sat in shock that Nick would say such a thing. I stood, ready to pounce on the jerk. I just needed to wait for the right word. Until then, I had to stay put, as ordered, no matter how much I wanted a pound of flesh from Nick.

"I want to kill you for what you've done!" Nick screamed.

Like he'd wanted to kill Molly for firing Erika? Interesting choice of words.

"Fix this!" Erika yelled. "Fix it now, Annabelle!"

"Oh, my gosh!" Annabelle said. "Would you two just calm down? This is getting out of hand. Of course I can fix it, if you, like, sit down, shut up and give me a chance to do so!"

Silence fell over the store except for someone's heavy breathing. I imagined it to be Nick's.

"This is going to soothe it," Annabelle said, her voice calm. "I'll give you some to take home, and you'll be all better in an hour or two, tops."

"An hour or two?!" Erika screeched. "I can't walk around like this for an hour or two!"

"No, she can't," Nick growled. "Fix it so she looks better *now*."

My phone buzzed in my pocket. I pulled it out to find Trevor calling me. I let it go to voicemail and typed: *Can't talk.*

I received a note back.

Where are you?

What part of 'can't talk' didn't he understand?

Sage Advice. Can't talk.

I shoved my phone in my pocket even though it vibrated again. No time for texting.

Nick continued to yell at Annabelle while Erika cried.

"If you can stop crying, then the salve would have a chance of staying on your face," Annabelle said.

Suddenly, the sound of glass breaking filled the air. I gasped and fought the urge to look around the corner.

"What was that?" Daisy asked, her ears perked.

"I don't know," I whispered. "Go out there and find out."

She trotted out then came in quickly.

"Nick broke a table," she said. "He's mad. Erika looks ugly."

"Get out of my store!" Annabelle screeched. "You can't act like that in here!"

"Fix my girlfriend's face!" More glass breaking.

"Turnip! Turnip!" Annabelle yelled.

What the heck did that mean?

"I'm not walking around with her face looking like a pepperoni pizza," Nick raged. "If you don't fix her, I promise you, you'll regret it."

More glass shard tinkled to the floor. He was going to destroy Sage Advice.

"You listen here," Annabelle said. "You're treading on thin ice, killer. I'll put a bullet in you. The police are on the way."

"For what?!" he yelled. "Because you ruined my girlfriend and I broke some stuff? I should sue you!"

"Turnip! Turnip!"

Was it possible that Annabelle had become so upset, she'd forgotten the code word?

An ear-piercing scream filled the air and sent Daisy rushing up the stairs, followed by Jack.

"Run, Gina! Run!" she yelled. "Run as fast as your two legs can go, Gina!"

I couldn't sit back any longer, regardless of what Annabelle had instructed me to do.

After rounding the corner, I gasped at the sight before me. Erika held a glass jar she'd pulled from the wall above her head and then smashed it into a table.

"Turnip! Turnip!" Annabelle screamed.

I sprang into action. The enraged Erika was so focused on Annabelle, she didn't see me while she picked another jar from the wall. When I grabbed her around the waist and pushed her to the side, she turned while Annabelle scrambled behind the cash register.

Erika faced me, and I gasped. Goodness, what in the world had Annabelle done to her?

Large red welts littered her cheeks while her nose and forehead were covered in white salve. With her wide eyes, dilated pupils and bared teeth, she looked savage.

And scary as heck.

She lunged at me, and I was so taken aback by her face, I froze. Thankfully, my survival instincts kicked in and I stepped to the side. She flew by me and I jumped on her back, then we fell to the floor. The glass jar crashed and its herbal content scattered across the tile.

Annabelle came to my side with a zip tie. "Why in the world do you have one of these?"

I asked as I quickly captured Erika's hands behind her back.

"I also have a knife, bear spray and extra bullets," Annabelle said. "I like to be prepared."

Standing, I turned to Nick.

With his mouth hanging open, he was slowly backing toward the door.

"Sit down!" I yelled. "Right where you are!"

To my surprise, he pushed his hair out of his face and did as he was told, right in the middle of the store.

Annabelle ran to the front door and locked it. It was then that I realized my heart might burst from my chest and I was sweating buckets. Nothing was going as we'd planned. These two were supposed to be upset, leave, and then Nick was to come back after dark and try to kill Annabelle. That's when we'd catch him.

"What took you so long?!" she yelled.

"You told me to come when I heard *avocado*, not *turnip*!"

Her face fell. "Oh. I guess I, like, got confused."

"It appears that way," I grumbled. Placing my hands on my knees, I took a few deep breaths, then stood upright and turned to Nick. "Do I need to tie you up as well, or are you going to stop breaking things and yelling?"

"No, ma'am," he said. "You don't need to tie me up. I'm good right here."

Erika had sat herself up and leaned against the counter, tears streaming down her face. I'd been so convinced Nick was the killer, but now I wasn't so sure. I'd never seen such a violent side of Erika. Maybe it had been her all along.

No sense beating around the bush. "Which one of you killed Molly?"

They met each other's gaze, then stared at me. Silence.

"The police are on their way," I lied. "You're going to have to confess at some point."

"He did it," Erika spat. "I saw him at the end of the hallway when I left after begging Molly for my job back."

I turned to Nick, whose eyes were wide in surprise. "I... I didn't kill anyone!"

Believing him was difficult, especially after the behavior I'd witnessed and the things Erika had shared on her TikTok channel and with me personally. Although he always said he had Erika's best interest at heart and he wanted her happy, he was a controlling, manipulative jerk. But did that make him a killer?

"Let me ask you this," I said. "You love Erika, right?"

He glanced at her, and doubt flickered across his face. "Yes, but not looking like that."

Shaking my head, I bent down in front of him. "Let me tell you something, you superficial turd. You will end up alone in life if you don't change your ways. You'll be the saddest, most pathetic old man this town has ever seen. Don't you forget that."

I stood and walked over to Erika. "You said he killed Molly. Do you know what happened?"

She shook her head. "I just know that I thought I saw a man there, and now you're saying one of us did it. It wasn't me, so it must be him."

Maybe I'd been wrong about this whole situation. Perhaps Trevor had been right and Lewis was the killer. These two just seemed so... innocent right now.

But the evidence. I decided to ask about the evidence.

"Why did you take down the video of you with the pink hammer?" I asked Erika.

She narrowed her gaze. "What are you talking about?"

"There was a video on your TikTok channel of you using a pink hammer to pound a nail into the wall. In it, you spoke about pretending to hit someone who had done you wrong when slamming the nail."

The color drained from her face. "I don't even know what video you're talking about. And I want to leave right now. I'm going to sue Annabelle and ruin her life for making my face look like this. And maybe you, too, Gina. I can't believe you're in on this."

"You just trashed my store, young lady," Annabelle yelled. "You want to sue me because I tried to help you with your horrible pores? Do you *really* want those revealed in a courtroom?"

"Okay, enough," I sighed. "One of you killed Molly and we're going to sit here until the killer is revealed. I don't have anything else to do today."

"I thought you said the police were on their way," Nick said.

Shoot. I'd forgotten about that.

"They are," I replied. "But you two sit there in silence for much longer, and I promise you, you'll both go to jail until the police sort it out."

"Just admit it, Nick!" Erika screamed. "You did it!"

He cursed under his breath then shook his head. "I knew you were a psycho. I wasn't there, Erika. You can tell anyone you want that you saw me there, but I wasn't."

"Then where were you?" Annabelle asked.

He stared at her a long moment, then his gaze fell to the floor. Silence blanketed the room.

"Are you having an affair?" Erika whispered.

For a second, his breath caught. Had Erika seen it? Based on the way she screamed at the top of her lungs, I took it as a definitive yes.

"I knew it," she said, once again crying hysterically. "I didn't want to face it, but I knew it. Who is she?"

"So, you, like, have an alibi for the night Molly was killed?" Annabelle asked.

Nick nodded just as a tapping sound came from the front door. I glanced over my shoulder to find Trevor, his brow furrowed. Annabelle hurried over and unlocked it, and Trevor slowly walked in, taking in the scene. "What the heck is going on here?"

"Look what they did to my face!" Erika yelled. "And they've tied me up!"

"Well, you shouldn't have thrown your little hissy fit in my store," Annabelle grumbled.

Trevor glanced over at me.

"One of them killed Molly," I said. "I'm positive of it, but I can't get them to admit it."

"So, you... what did you two do?"

I pulled him to the side. "Annabelle and I were thinking that if Nick was the killer, he'd lose his mind with his girlfriend looking so bad. He says he wants her happy. Did he kill Molly in the hopes Erika would get her job back? Or to instigate some type of revenge for Molly upsetting Erika when she fired her?"

"And why is Erika tied up?" he asked, crossing his arms over his chest. "And why does her face look like someone set it on fire?"

I glanced over my shoulder. I was going to argue with the analogy, but dang it, he was right. "It was our way of poking Nick to see what his reaction would be."

"So you were hoping to get him riled up enough that maybe he'd try to kill you or something?"

When he put it that way, the idea sounded downright dumb and dangerous. Embarrassment warmed my cheeks. "Something like that."

He chuckled and shook his head. "Baiting a killer is a terrible plan, Gina, but in a way I'm glad you did."

"Why?"

"I spoke to Lewis about his phone being at the scene of the crime. He said he couldn't find it before he left the store that evening. We were able to get some prints off it, and

Erika had clearly handled it. We figure she stole his phone and hid it at the store as a way to frame him for the killing."

With a gasp, I turned to her. I felt bad for her, but at the same time, I was relieved it seemed the case was finally over.

"So, before she left, she took Lewis' phone and hid it somewhere in the store. Then she returned and begged Molly for her job back, and if she didn't get it, she had a plan."

"Yes. Get rid of Molly. She figured Lewis would hire her back."

"But what about beyond that? She had to know that the phone she planted would frame Lewis."

Erika stared at me a long moment. "If he went to prison, then he'd get what he deserved for letting that cow fire me."

"What are you saying?!" Nick yelled. "You killed Molly?!"

"Why do you care, you cheating jerk," Erika mumbled. "You were with that tramp that night when I needed you the most! I hate you!"

As the tears flowed down her cheeks, I felt

sorry for her, but at the same time, she scared me. I couldn't imagine killing someone over a job, but I could now see that I wasn't dealing with someone mentally stable.

Daisy slowly walked into the room, trailed by Jack. "I was right, Gina. This was a bad idea, but at least Bloody Boots finally got hers!"

CHAPTER 20

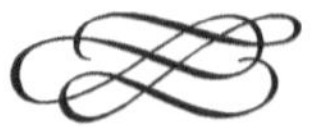

THE NEXT DAY, I drove Frank and Marilyn to Fiona Wellington's home, which was just outside Flagstaff. Despite the cold, the Department of Transportation had done a wonderful job of keeping the roads clear and ice-free, which I appreciated.

I hoped with every fiber of my being the dogs and Fiona would be a match. If so, I'd be able to call my son, Jacob, who resided at the college, and meet him for lunch. Daisy would never forgive me since Jacob was one of her favorite people, but I'd had to leave her at home. The last thing I needed was a dog fight in the car while driving. Unfortunately, she just couldn't seem to keep to herself. Perhaps

I'd keep mum about my visit with Jacob, if I was lucky enough to see him.

Google Maps led me to a tidy brown house with dark brown trim. The front yard was gated with a white picket fence. With it being the dead of winter, patches of brown grass showed through the snow, but the path had been shoveled. Along the front of the house sat empty flowerbeds. I imagined them full of daffodils and petunias in the spring and summer.

As I shut off the car, the front door opened. A tall, thin woman with long gray hair, wearing a dark blue parka, jeans and black boots stepped out onto the porch, smiled, and waved.

"Okay, guys," I said to the dogs. "Please let me know if you like her, okay?"

Although I wanted the dogs gone and sanity to be restored to my home, I didn't want to put them somewhere they wouldn't be happy. Daisy had shared long ago that it wasn't the human who picked the dog, but the dog who picked the human. If the homeless pet met a human they liked, they'd do something like lick their hand, or nuzzle their lap, maybe even give them a quick kiss. If they weren't interested, they ignored the human.

I exited the car and waved, then opened the back door to leash them. They led the way up the pathway and approached Fiona slowly.

"My goodness," she said. "Aren't you two a handsome couple?" She then greeted me. "Hello, Gina. It's lovely to meet you."

I shook her hand and grinned, liking her immediately. "Likewise."

"Shall we go inside to get acquainted and out of this bitter cold?"

"I'd very much appreciate that."

Once we were in the house and we'd shucked our coats, she offered me tea. How very British of her. Tea was not my thing, so I declined.

"May we let them off leash?" she asked once we were situated in the comfortable living room furnished in taupe and rust colors.

"Of course." I unclipped them and they began to explore the space.

"Where were they found?" Fiona asked.

"Sedona," I said. "Their owner passed

away and they were put with a rescue organization there. One of the rescue's volunteers was housing them, but his mother called and suggested he come home for a few days because of a sick relative, so he asked me to watch them."

"Brilliant man," Fiona said. "When mother 'suggests' something, it's always a smart idea to follow her advice."

I laughed and nodded. "That's exactly what I told him."

"Let me tell you a little more about myself," she said. "I'm sixty-seven years old. I obviously live alone with my husband and dog now gone." She shook her head. "It's been an absolutely terrible year."

"I'm sorry for your loss," I said.

"Thank you. Anyway, I walk five miles a day, unless the streets aren't plowed. The dogs would obviously come with me." She sighed, her smile fading. "I do have friends and like spending time with them, but here at home, I'm terribly lonely."

When Jacob had moved out, I felt that hole in my heart. It was getting easier, especially with Daisy around always talking to me.

Well, I hoped she was actually speaking to me and I wasn't hearing voices.

I wanted to help Fiona and ease her loneliness, but I wouldn't leave the dogs in a place they didn't want to be. My loyalty was to them, no matter how difficult it had been having them at my house.

"Do you two loves want to stay with me?" Fiona asked. She held her hand out to Marilyn, who was slowly approaching her. Internally, I cringed and hoped Frank wouldn't jump in and bare his teeth or growl.

Instead, he also approached. Marilyn allowed Fiona to gently run her hand over her head while Frank stayed at Marilyn's flank. My breath caught in my throat as Fiona whispered sweet nothings to Marilyn. When the dog's tail began to wag, it gave a satisfying slap to Frank's little brown face.

"She's so sweet," Fiona said as Marilyn licked her fingers.

The breath I'd been holding slowly released when Frank walked around Marilyn and vied for Fiona's attention. He stretched up to lick Marilyn's jaw, then Fiona's hand.

My goodness. Tears welled in my eyes. Did we have a match?

I glanced at Fiona to find tears in her eyes as well. "I'm chuffed to have dogs around again."

"They seem happy to be here," I replied. I watched the three of them for a few more minutes, then Frank jumped on the couch and curled up next to Fiona. The last of my worries slipped away. The dogs were letting me know they'd found their person.

"I'd like to take them in," Fiona said eagerly. "They're just lovely."

One more concern needed to be addressed. "Do you have a fenced backyard?"

"Of course. Let me show you."

I followed her through the dining room to a sliding glass door. The large snow-covered yard held many trees and would be nicely shaded in the summer. It seemed like the perfect setup. The dogs would be exercised regularly. Most importantly, they seemed to enjoy Fiona.

Turning to her, I smiled. "If you'd like to take them, I think they'd be very happy here."

"Wonderful." She clapped her hands together at her chest, her smile wide. "Do you have papers for me to sign?"

We returned to the living room and I pulled out the adoption agreement I'd stuffed into my purse before leaving. We went over the terms, which basically said the dogs were healthy, they had all their shots, and if for some reason Fiona decided they weren't going to work out, she needed to phone me or Corey from the Sedona rescue. We discussed food and eating schedules. She was excited to go buy some new dog beds.

When everything was signed and she'd paid the adoption fee, I said goodbye to the dogs, then took my leave. Neither tried to follow me, which only solidified they were in the right place.

As I pulled away from the house, I sighed with relief. I picked up the phone and dialed my son.

"Hey, Mom. What's up?"

"I'm about ten minutes away from the school. Do you want to have lunch?"

"Heck, yes!" he said. "I'm starving!"

I smiled. "Meet me in the west parking lot and think about where you want to go."

"Sounds good. See you in a few."

When I found him in the parking lot, I received the best hug ever, and I couldn't wipe the smile from my face.

Lunch was us catching up over burgers and fries. I told him about the murder, the investigation, and finally nailing the killer.

"You're the coolest mom ever," he said, shaking his head. "Wait until I tell my roommates about this. I'm so impressed."

"Well, if I'm the coolest mom ever, you know what that makes you, right?"

He threw his head back and laughed. "The coolest kid?"

"Exactly."

Time flew by way too fast, and he had to get to his next class. Although I was tempted to tell him to skip it so I could have more time with him, I bit my tongue to keep my mouth shut.

"I'm coming home for Spring Break," he said. "Is that okay?"

"Of course it is. No big trips with your friends?" I asked, very pleased with this new development.

"Nah. None of us can afford to go anywhere, so we'll hang out around here. There's plenty of fun things to do."

I tried to contain my excitement. My son home for a week? I couldn't wait! Hopefully, his plans would remain unchanged.

After we said goodbye, I headed home, my heart filled with love. My son was the thing in my life that made me most proud. We'd been through some pretty difficult times, but he'd grown up to become one heck of a nice guy. Although I may be biased, I also found him smart, confident and terribly good-looking. I couldn't wait to see what his future held.

EPILOGUE

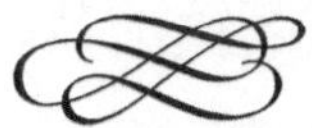

Spring Break

I DIDN'T KNOW what time it was when I heard someone pounding on my front door, but I was determined to ignore them. Until Daisy began to bark.

"Get up, Gina!" she yelled as she carried on. "There's a serial killer at the door!"

"Really?" I grumbled, throwing back the covers. "I don't think serial killers announce their presence."

"That's probably true. But what if it's Jacob?" she said, jumping from the bed. "Maybe he forgot his keys!"

In my sleepiness, I'd forgotten that he was

home for Spring Break. I sprang up, grabbed my glasses and hurried to the front door. After checking the porch through the window, I saw that it was Trevor.

That uneasy feeling I'd had the previous evening became so heavy, my legs seemed to be made of cement as I opened the door.

"Trevor! Trevor!" Daisy yelled, dancing around his feet. "Trevor, pet me!"

"What happened?" I asked. As I studied his face, I noted the serious scowl. His hands clenched at his sides while his shoulders bunched under his uniform.

"I've been trying to call you," he said gruffly. "I need to come in."

Stepping aside, I said, "I didn't hear the phone."

I shut the door and he took me into a long embrace. Tears welled in my eyes, even though I had no idea what he was about to say. Whatever it was, I understood it would alter my existence. I pulled away, hoping it had nothing to do with my son.

"What happened?" I asked again, crossing my arms over my chest.

"Let's sit down."

"No. Tell me right now."

He sighed and ran his thumb between his eyebrows. Finally, he met my gaze. "Gina, there's been a murder."

Oh, no. Where was Jacob? What time was it? I glanced out the window and noted the sun was on the horizon, almost ready to make its debut for the day.

He had left the previous evening for a night out with friends. He'd apparently been out all night, or...

I had to force myself to ask the question and I was terrified of what the response would be. "Is... is Jacob dead?" I always imagined I'd know if my son was no longer with me. I felt such an intricate connection to him, surely I'd instinctively be aware of his death.

"No! No," he said, placing his hands on my shoulders. "Jacob is... Jacob's down at the emergency clinic sleeping off one heck of a bender."

Relief flooded through me, but it only brought on more questions. Unless something had drastically changed, my son wasn't a big drinker. "What does that mean?"

"They couldn't wake him at the party, so they took him to the clinic."

Bile rose in my throat. "Is he okay?"

"They say he's going to be just fine, but he's in trouble."

I furrowed my brow. "Why is he in trouble?"

"Look, Gina. Here's the deal. Last night there was a big house party out at the Willard place. When the kids came to this morning, they found a young woman dead. She'd been strangled."

I nodded, the pain of a young life lost lancing through me. But that didn't explain why my son was in trouble. "What does that have to do with Jacob?"

"He... he was found passed out next to her with a rope in his hand."

The room began to spin. I grabbed the wall to steady myself.

"Jacob wouldn't do anything like that," Daisy said. I glanced down to find her at my feet. "Jacob is a good dog, like me."

"What... what does that mean?" I asked, meeting Trevor's gaze.

He shrugged and ran a hand through his

blond hair. "It means that Sheriff Mallory thinks she's got the killer."

Rage exploded within me with such force, I saw stars before my eyes while I continued to grip the wall. "Jacob had nothing to do with this," I hissed.

"I'm sure he didn't," Trevor said evenly. "But Mallory thinks he did and I wanted to be the one to tell you what was going on."

"Gina, you have to help Jacob," Daisy said.

"I want to see my son," I growled.

"You can see him when he wakes up."

"No. Now."

I marched down the hallway and quickly changed into a pair of jeans and sweatshirt, then I grabbed my sneakers and returned to Trevor.

"I want to see Jacob and then I'm going to find out who's responsible for this tragedy, because it isn't my son."

"It's probably best if you stay out of it."

"No! Mallory will happily railroad him and I'm not going to allow that to happen! Now, you either take me to the emergency clinic or I'm driving myself!"

My voice had taken on a high-pitched tone of complete panic and my hands began to shake. If I was going to help Jacob, I needed to reign in my anxiety. The tears I held back wouldn't do him any good. To save him, I needed to take action.

"Gina, you need to let me do my job," he said softly.

"Listen up, Trevor." I pointed a shaky finger at him. "You're either going to help me, or you're going to get out of my way. There is *nothing*, I repeat, *nothing*, that I won't do to clear my son. Do you understand me?"

WHAT LENGTHS WILL Gina go to in order to clear Jacob of the murder? Find out in Puppy Love and Panic, which you can get directly from me at carlywintercozymysteries.com at lower price and before you get it on retailers

ALSO BY CARLY WINTER

The Heywood Hounds Cozy Mysteries

(Humorous cozy mysteries featuring a talking dog)

Amateur sleuth, Gina, and her talking dog, Daisy, solve murders in the small town of Heywood, Arizona.

The Heywood Herbalist Cozy Mysteries

(Small town contemporary cozies)

From Hollywood, California, to Heywood, Arizona, trouble follows her...

After her husband's brutal killing and her fall from the Hollywood elite, the disgraced Samantha Rathbone moves to Heywood, Arizona, hoping to forget her past and live a quiet life of anonymity.

It doesn't go as planned.

Sedona Spirt Mysteries

(Paranormal cozies)

Bernie and the ghost of her dead grandmother find themselves in the middle of various murder investigations. Danger and hilarity ensues as the crazy duo follow the clues to discover the killers.

The Tri-Town Murders

(Small town contemporary cozies)

Follow newspaper reporter Tilly and her group of fun, quirky friends as they solve murders in a fictional, small town in California.

ABOUT THE AUTHOR

USA Today bestselling author Carly Winter writes fun, small town cozy mysteries, always with a dash of humor and quirky characters. When not writing, you can find her spending time with her family, on a Pilates reformer or enjoying the fantastic Arizona weather (except summer - she doesn't like summer). She does like dogs, wine and chocolate and wishes Christmas happened twice a year.

To be notified of new releases, book recommendations, to learn more about Carly and for your chance to win giveaways, please visit: CarlyWinterCozyMysteries.com